Hill Hawk Hattie

Hill Hawk
Hattie

Clara Gillow Clark

CANDLEWICK PRESS
CAMBRIDGE, MASSACHUSETTS

Copyright © 2003 by Clara Gillow Clark

First edition 2003

Library of Congress Cataloging-in-Publication Data

Clark, Clara Gillow.
Hill Hawk Hattie / Clara Gillow Clark. — 1st ed.
p. cm.
Summary: Angry and lonely after her mother dies, eleven-year-old
Hattie pretends to be a boy and joins her father on an adventure-
filled rafting trip down the Delaware River in the late 1800s to
transport logs from New York to Philadelphia.
ISBN 0-7636-1963-9
[1. Fathers and daughters — Fiction. 2. Death — Fiction.
3. Sex role — Fiction. 4. Rafting (Sports) — Fiction. 5. Logging —
Fiction. 6. Mountain life — Fiction.] I. Title.
PZ7.C5415 Fl 2003
[Fic] — dc21   2002073740

2 4 6 8 10 9 7 5 3 1

Printed in the United States of America

This book was typeset in Stempel Schneidler.

Candlewick Press
2067 Massachusetts Avenue
Cambridge, Massachusetts 02140

visit us at www.candlewick.com

For my niece
Lisa Stanton Hoover
in loving memory

Hill Hawk Hattie

PART I

≈ The Cabin ≈

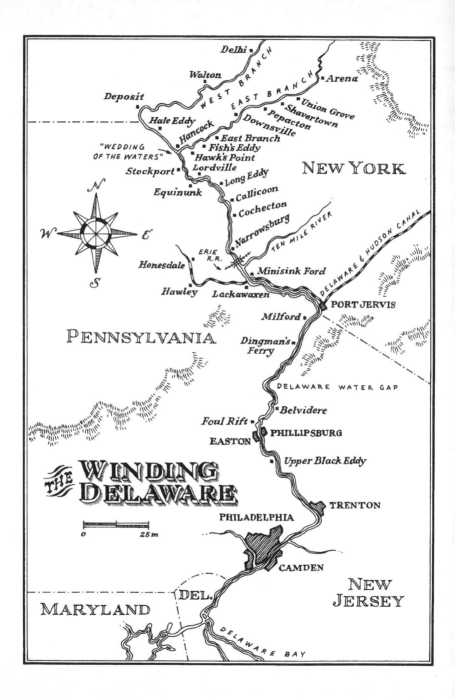

THE WINDING DELAWARE

Chapter One

Ma died in November. Now it's just me and Pa.

Pa said, "You have to do the cooking and fetching now, girl." That meant no more school.

That's about all he's said. Pa doesn't have much use for words. He's not particular fond of those who do. Guess he must hate my guts. Guess I'm not too fond of his. The way I see it, we're stuck.

Since I don't get to talk much, I've taken to writing things down: things I don't want to forget; things about Ma, mainly; and things about me, Hattie Basket; things that are starting to get erased like chalk from a slate board at school from living with Pa.

Pa used to call Ma and me *his* girls. Now, he just says "girl," orders me around with curse words like I'm nothing.

I'm not nothing, though, 'cause I feel too mean inside to be that.

Pa goes off every morning to work in the woods, felling trees with axes and crosscut saws, chopping out the tops and trimming off the limbs, hewing them into logs to raft down the Delaware to Philadelphia come spring when the ice breaks up. He likes to work. Since Ma died, he likes to drink hard, too.

I stay at home and learn to do the rest — split the wood and put it in the wood box; keep the fire; bake bread, johnnycake, biscuits, and pandowdy with the apples Ma dried last fall; milk the cow; separate the milk; churn the cream into butter; fork down hay from the mow; muck the stall; haul water from the spring; do the mending; clean and skin rabbits, squirrels, and other varmints that Pa kills. I can make a stew but not squirrel or rabbit pie like Pa wants. There's not much I do right; maybe, nothing. Guess I do burn the biscuits on the bottom pretty near every time.

The beginning of March I told Pa that my birthday was coming. I said that I'd be eleven on the thirteenth of March. I told him I'd outgrown my dress. Said I'd favor me some hair ribbons, too. Purple would be nice, I said. Purple was Ma's favorite color — purple like the dark violets that grew in the deep woods or like the sweet plums from her special tree or like the purple ribbon of sky after sunset in winter.

But all Pa did was grunt.

Come my birthday, Pa got home late, smelling of whiskey, a brown jug under one arm, a brown parcel under the other. He tossed the package on the table. Inside were overalls, a red flannel shirt, and long johns from the general store in Pepacton.

I searched everywhere inside that brown wrapper for purple ribbons. There was nothing but boy stuff.

Guess Pa knew what I was looking for all right. "Don't feel right buying girl stuff," he said, looking away from me.

I scowled. Didn't *want* to buy girl stuff anymore is what he meant.

Pa laughed. "You're tall and scrawny like a boy; might as well dress like one."

I laughed, too, though I did not see the joke. Only thing to do when Pa was acting happy drunk. Acting happy didn't come natural to Pa anymore. Didn't come natural to me, either.

Pa reached in the pocket of his wool coat and pulled out a small bag with peppermint sticks. We each had half of one after supper.

We sucked on them in silence for the longest time; the strong taste of peppermint burned my throat and nostrils in the most delicious way. Outside, it started to snow, the wind swirling clouds of white stuff against the cabin window, howling that winter was not about to leave any too soon.

"Snowed like this when you was born," Pa said, sucking now on a rotted tooth.

I wanted him to keep talking. But he didn't. He had a look of pain on his face. Might have been from the hole in his tooth, might have been that he was missing Ma the way I did every single second. Whatever ailed him, he doused it good with whiskey from his jug.

"Like me to read the Bible?" Ma used to read aloud sometimes. Pa couldn't read much, had no desire to do more than write his name.

Pa shook his head.

"How 'bout the almanac?"

"Ayah," he said.

I read the weather and moon phases for March and April. I knew Pa was anxious for winter to break so he could build a raft of logs and ride the river again. Pa loved to raft. He said it was like one long and thrilling sleigh ride, said the hard part was walking back up the hills again once he got to the end of the river ride. Said he was mighty glad he didn't have to pull the raft back up with him.

Pa listened close for a while. Then he dozed off, snoring in his chair. I kept on reading, switching to the Bible till the lamp sputtered and the fire burned so low the cold crept in through every crack, wrapped itself around me like a cloak of ice.

The next morning, I put on my new clothes, rolling up the pant legs on the overalls. When I came down from the loft, it was still dark. I lit the lamp, caught sight of myself in the windowpane. Pa was right. I looked like a boy except for my long braids.

Folk always said that I had Pa's strong chin, plain face, and nut-brown hair. Never knew what they meant by that, exactly. Pa had so many whiskers you could barely see his face, couldn't see his chin a'tall. Ma told me not to mind the simple-minded. Ma said I would get my girl looks in due time. "You'll be a pretty girl, Hattie Belle."

But I looked like a boy now with no sign I could tell of ever changing. And even less a chance of ever getting a new dress or ribbons for my hair. Didn't have time to comb it; couldn't braid proper anyhow. My hair just got more snarled and troublesome by the day. Dumb hair. Before I could stop myself, I grabbed up Ma's shears and cut off one of my braids.

I looked at that soft rope of hair in my hands and swallowed a whole lot of sorriness. A quiver went clear through me, but I didn't cry. It was too late for that. I took Ma's shears and cut off the other braid. I built up the fire then and made griddlecakes and home fries and put on the coffeepot.

Pa got up when he smelled breakfast, blinked when he saw me with my hair chopped off. Didn't say a word, just nodded like it suited him fine.

Guess a girl was too much bother for Pa. Maybe he'd like it better now if I was his boy. I didn't mind keeping my girl feelings hidden away for a time, but I didn't want to be a plain old scrawny boy, nohow.

Chapter Two

After Pa left for the woods, I went up the ladder to the loft and hid my braids under the mattress ticking. I took out Ma's diary I kept hidden under there.

The diary was the one Ma was writing in when she died. Ma never did write much, mostly one line about chores, my chores now. The diary fell open by itself to the page I'd thumbed a bushel of times. *Hattie Belle won the spelling bee at school for the second time,* Ma wrote in the month of April.

Ma didn't keep accurate dates. She didn't write every day, either, just moved on to the next clean page. I knew the spelling bee was in May before school was out. No matter. I liked to run my fingers over her words. I could almost think her alive again.

Ma left nearly a whole diary of blank white pages. I suppose a preacher person might say it was wrong, but I knew Ma would think it just fine if I wrote my own words in her book. I was careful what I put down, and I wrote scrunching my words together so I didn't fill up the pages too fast. I didn't write about my chores, and I didn't say one thing mean about Pa even if I was burning up hot like a cherry log crackling in the stove.

Today, I wrote to Ma about things I didn't understand. Like why Pa doesn't call me his girl anymore, and why he's taken to cussing so much and drinking hard. Pa was never much of a talker, but he never used to mind if Ma and me talked. Seems like it's only my chatter he despises. Or, maybe, it's me. I tried talking to God but it didn't work. I could talk to him day and night; didn't seem to mind my chattering the way Pa did. Trouble was, God was no different than Pa when it came to answering back.

Ma always told me the answers if she knew them. Mornings before school, she'd gently brush the snarls from my long hair and braid it up again, listening and pondering and telling me everything she knew about animals and weather and such.

Afternoons, when I got home from school, I helped

her with chores and told her all I learned in school. Didn't tell her how I got picked on for being a Hill Hawk with a crazy Ma, though. I asked Pa once why we were called that. He said he didn't rightly know. Guessed hawks were loners and liked to nest in high places instead of down in the pretty little valleys where everybody stuck together like pitch to a pine tree. That made good sense. I knew Hill Hawks didn't go to church or socials. Mostly, they didn't bother to send their children to school and nobody bothered them about it. I was the only Hill Hawk to attend school real regular. Ma insisted on that.

I learned not to fight, 'cause Ma worried that I was being scrappy for fun and that was not proper or lady-like. Didn't want to worry Ma.

Pretty near everyone at school was children of farmers from the hollow north of us. They shied away from me like I had some sort of pox, but I didn't care. I could run faster, spell, memorize and recite better, and do ciphering in my head. In the winter when the snow was deep, Ma kept me home and taught me things that weren't in my schoolbooks, like the Latin names of wildflowers and trees and how to be a real lady.

Being home with Ma and having Pa come home cheer-ful was the best. Guess Ma was the sugar that kept us sweet. Now she's gone, and Pa isn't cheerful. Can't think of one good reason to be a Hill Hawk.

What I wanted to know was why God took her away and left me alone with Pa. Wanted to know why I was so ornery feeling, and why I wasn't getting my girl looks yet. Wished I'd taken after Ma — soft and pretty, dainty as a teacup and sweet as plum pudding.

Please, Ma, I wrote. *If you could show me a sign, something I can see, something to keep me from being so ornery feeling inside, something to help me understand Pa, it'd be a great help. I got mad and cut off my braids. Awful sorry about that. Pa seems to like it. . . .*

I pressed my lips together and scowled to keep from writing any meanness about him.

Pa brought me some peppermint sticks for my birthday. I didn't mention the boy's clothing or that he was drunk on red-eye again. Feeling righteous, I slid the diary back under the ticking and scooted down the ladder. Chores would wait but not without somehow accumulating bother and trouble.

I built up the fire and filled the wood box, mixed the bread before going out to the barn. I expected to hear the cow complaining when I slid back the door, but for once she was quiet. Ma named her Blossom, but I've taken to calling her Briar, 'cause she'd gotten mean since Ma wasn't around to milk her and spoil her with sweet talk and hay drizzled with blackstrap molasses.

That cow riled me, swatted at me with her tail, tried to kick the milk bucket, moved so the milk squirted somewhere besides the pail. Me and old Briar had a tussle every day — if she kicked me, I kicked her; if she swatted me with her filthy tail, I swatted her hard on the behind. Sometimes, I hit her first.

But today, I was determined to be patient, for Ma. I was, too, till I walked in and saw lazy old Briar lying down. I kicked her in the behind. "Get your lazy arse up," I hollered.

But Briar didn't budge. "Come on, Bossy." I pushed against her side. Briar didn't push back. "Blossom, please get up. Please." But she didn't get up. She couldn't get up. She was dead.

I dropped to my knees in the hay by her side and threw myself against her bony flank. "Please don't be dead, Blossom." I bawled like a dumb sissy, but it didn't help anything. Pa would probably think I killed her. The surly way he acted these days, he might decide to whup me. No more milk for dumplings or mush, no sweet cream for butter.

I dragged my sorry self back to the cabin; took out Ma's diary again. I wrote, *On March 14, 1883, Hattie Belle Basket kicked a dead cow.* I figured I'd best be more careful about asking Ma for any sort of sign again. Guess Ma showed me. Guess if Pa whupped me it wouldn't be as much trouble as another sign from Ma.

I fretted about it all day. What was I going to say to Pa when he got home? Better to feed him first. Not say a single word till he got drowsy. Ma had a charming way of talking, and she could bake sweet plum pies with a flaky crust. I couldn't do either. Pa used to whistle like a hawk, high and shrill and long, soon as he reached the clearing. I'd whistle back and take off running down the path to meet him, carry his dinner bucket, and grab his hand. Not anymore. Now, I wasn't so tickled to see him.

On days when Ma was making those sweet plum pies, I'd ask her to tell me again about her plum tree, and everything else. "Your pa bought me that tree as a wedding gift," she'd say with a secret sort of smile that showed how much she loved him.

That's when she would tell me about Kingston, where she'd lived in a grand house, wore pretty dresses, had servants to take care of everything. It sounded like a fairy tale. Ma didn't have one fine thing to show me from that other life, except her ownself.

"Tell me again how you met Pa," I'd say.

And Ma would tell me while she mixed the crust and rolled it out, filled the plates with the cooked plums, and put the pies in the oven. "Before the Erie Railroad came through Hancock," she'd begin, and I'd sit quiet and listen, "it was quicker for the river men to come back to the hills by New York City. They'd take the train from Trenton to the Hudson River, ferry across to the city, take the night boat to Kingston, and walk clear over the Catskill Mountains to Pepacton.

"But while they waited for the night boat, those men got a shave and a bath and went shopping for ready-made suits at a department store. What a grand sight they made, piling into Kingston dressed in frock coats. I spotted your pa as soon as he walked into the hotel dance one warm spring night. He was tall and lovely and quiet.

"Wild boy, they called him. Not for drinking or fighting, though he could do that when he had a mind to, but because he raised himself, lived alone in the woods right here after his folk died of some sort of fever. He was special, Hattie Belle. He was a fine dancer, knew how to sing, how to love a girl just right," she'd say, her voice going soft.

Then I'd ask, "Will we ever go to Kingston?"

"It's a world away, Hattie Belle."

"Too far for us to travel?"

"Too far forever and ever," she'd say.

Guess I never would know my kinfolk. It was strange thinking how Ma had a whole life I couldn't make a real picture of in my head.

"Maybe, you shouldn't have left Kingston with Pa," I'd say to test her. "Maybe, you should've stayed where you had fine things."

"Not as fine as you and Pa," Ma would say. "Not as fine as having you and Pa to love me." The way Ma smiled and brushed her hands over my cheeks, cupped my chin and kissed my hair, I knew she meant it. But Ma wore sadness often enough. It hung on her like a big, heavy coat that she wouldn't take off. I guess she missed her old life all right, or, maybe, it was just her ma that she was missing. Guess that's what it had to be all right. No matter what Ma said, the way I saw it, she got a raw deal — poor cabin in the woods, and no prettiness to gaze on but her plum tree in blossom.

Now things were different. When Pa came in from the woods, he did not whistle like a hawk or smile, so I did not whistle back or hurry out to meet him. I tried to keep my chipmunk chatter in my head, but some days I thought I would bust if I didn't get some of the words out. It's not fit to bring to mind the cussing that came out of Pa's mouth when I did that.

I grew bold as the day wore on, even bolder when I punched and kneaded the bread dough. I'd threaten Pa, that's what I'd do if he so much as thought about whupping me. I'm running away, I'd tell him. You'll just have to fix your own vittles and darn your own smelly socks from now on. I'm done.

My heart thumped like a dog scratching its fleas when it got close to dark, close to Pa coming home. Now don't chatter, Hattie Belle, I told myself.

Pa came home looking surly. Nearly died of fright just to look at his sour puss, corners of his mouth turned down, lower lip stuck out like he was aiming to pick a fight. Seeing as how I was the only one around, reckoned my chances were poor. Didn't have to worry about chipmunk chatter, though. That big talk of mine got stuck in my throat like a piece of jerky swallowed the wrong way.

"Where's the milk?" Pa growled.

"Blossom's dried up," I said, looking down, paying particular attention to my plate.

"Goldarnit, what did you do to her?"

"Nothing," I said, looking up. I stared him straight in the face, balled my hands into fists. "I didn't touch the mangy good-for-nothing cow. So don't be accusing me of something that's not my fault!"

Pa leaned toward me like he was going to grab me out of my chair. When Pa was in one of his surly moods, didn't matter what I did, I was bound to catch some cuss words or get cuffed a little before the night was over.

I got up, walked around the table to where he was sitting. "Might as well cuff me, if you're going to."

Pa stood up, way up. Yanked me off the floor like I was a floppy rag doll, held me in the air with one arm. I held my breath and bit my lip. Guessed I was going to get more than cuffed.

But he didn't hit me. Pa's shoulders started to shake, then he bust out laughing. Put me back down, sat down his ownself, and laughed till tears ran into his whiskers.

I stared at him warylike, 'cause I reckoned he could go back to his usual surly self at any second. He didn't.

"I known all along about the dead cow."

I scowled. Didn't like being fooled, fretting myself half-sick all day, thinking I'd be blamed.

Pa pulled on his whiskers, pulling some thoughts out of himself, maybe. Figured I'd rather not know what he was devising.

"Luke got pneumonia; he ain't gonna make it," Pa said, looking temporarily sorrowful. Luke was a mangy old Hill Hawk bachelor. He scared Ma once coming to the cabin to get Pa. I was in school, so I never did get to meet him. I smelled him, though. His odor stayed around for a good long while. Ma was in a rattled state for days. Luke never made any more visits. Figured Ma's screaming cured him of that.

"Guess you better come in the woods with me starting tomorrow, work off some of that goldurn scrappiness. You ain't no cook, nohow, and the cow's dead." Pa laughed, slapping his knee.

I didn't intend to open my mouth, but I did. "You want me to be Luke?" I spluttered.

Pa chuckled. "I'm saying I need your help, girl. You strong enough to use a mallet?"

I flexed an arm. My muscle popped right up, round and hard as a cobblestone from chopping wood all winter. "I'm strong enough," I said. "But I don't smell bad."

"Guess I won't hold that against you any," Pa said, wiping a grin off his face with the back of his hand. "But you got to do whatever I tell you with none of your sassy mouth. No matter what I say, you got to go along with it, you hear?"

"Yup," I said with a scowl. I heard all right, but I didn't have to like it. Truth was, it got kind of lonesome being in the cabin all day. I'd always wanted to see Pa working, but Ma said it wasn't proper or safe for a lady to be with the men.

After Pa went to sleep that night, I took out Ma's diary. *I'm going to work with Pa tomorrow. I sure hope you aren't mad at me for not being more ladylike. I want to be a real girl, but it's no use. I don't even own me a proper dress anymore, thanks to Pa. It's too hard without you here to help me. You shouldn't have quit on me, Ma. I need you real bad.*

After I wrote that, I was angry at Ma for turning her head to the wall and giving up. Never felt that way before; knew it wasn't right. Funny how everything going wrong seemed like Ma's fault somehow — Ma, who'd never done a mean thing in her life except die.

Chapter Three

Mostly I wouldn't let myself think about Ma dying. Even though I didn't dwell on it, I was sore with the pain, sore like a thorn festering under the skin, swelling and red and infected with pus. A thorn could be gotten out, the sore healing quick enough, but Ma dying festered so bad I reckoned I'd bust someday. Me, Hattie Belle, *Splat!* all over.

Tonight, lying on my mattress in the loft, listening to the fire snap, Pa snore, and the March wind try to blow the roof off, I thought about Ma dying; thought about the stabbing pain in her side and her coughing spells. The coughing never seemed to stop. Sometimes, I put my hands over my ears or went outside to stack wood. I couldn't bear it.

I stayed home from school with her when she took a turn for the worse. I made a poultice, according to her directions, a paste of mustard and spices in a flannel bag to lay on her chest, brewed sassafras tea with honey. I did everything she said. And then she quit on me. Quit trying, though I begged her not to. She quit anyway. It was one morning after Pa left to go into the woods, and I'd gone out to the barn to learn how to milk her stubborn cow. Ma lay abed, turned her face to the wall. When I came back in with the milk, Ma's breathing had turned to a gurgle that strangled her to death.

Me, I didn't want to eat or smile or even talk for the longest time. I blamed Pa, though I knew it was not his fault, blamed him all the same, the way he blamed me, maybe, for not being sweet and pretty like Ma. Anyhow I looked at it, I was stuck like a pickle in a salty brine. Done for, that's what.

Next morning, Pa got up early, went outside without hollering for me. Guess I wouldn't be going into the woods after all. Guess Pa's whiskey altered his memory again.

I pulled on my overalls and skedaddled down the ladder. I built up the fire, put some fat to melt in the fry pan, started slicing in cold potatoes, put on the coffee, buttered bread, cut off thick slices of ham for the dinner pails.

Pa came back in, threw off his hat and coat. "Cow's gone," he said. Didn't dare ask him a thing about it. We ate in silence. I was too afraid to open my mouth. Didn't know what I would jog out of his memory.

When Pa got up from the table, he put on his coat, fished in one of his deep pockets, and pulled out a bearskin cap. "This here's my old hat. Best put it on." Pa held it out to me like he was offering me something special.

I didn't say a word, just put on that cap and got going.

PART II

⊰ The Woods ⊱

Chapter Four

That morning when we left the cabin, a soft rose draped across the horizon like a lady's sash, separating earth from sky. It was still plenty dark. The wind woke up, kicked a dusting of fresh snow into my face. It was cold for March, nipped right through my wool coat, turned my skin to goose flesh. My feet were heavy and cold as blocks of ice cut from the river. Already, I was thinking I would've been better off alone in a warm cabin than out here in the cold and wind.

I tramped along behind Pa, passed by the plum tree where Ma was buried. Didn't pause. Besides the wind, the only sound was the crunching of our boots till we reached the edge of the woods. Four crows flew up from the bare branches and squawked, their wings whooshing as they passed overhead.

I had half a mind to squawk and beat my arms up and down, too. I didn't. Wouldn't help me any. I couldn't fly away from trouble like a crow. Ma would hate Pa for taking me to work in the woods. I didn't hate him for that, but I hated him for being surly and for not buying me a dress. I didn't feel much kindness for Ma this morning, either.

What would Pa tell the men about me? What in tarnation would I do if I had private business to take care of? What would I do if they did their business in front of me? Lucky for me I didn't have to go much. Ma always said I had an iron constitution.

By the time we started down the mountain into the hemlock forest, I was plenty warm and tired of thinking. Guess maybe I was ready to work. It was some sight, too, coming up on all those felled giants, branches chopped, tops cut, wood chips littering the packed-down snow, stumps poking up all over. Looked like hundreds of felled hemlocks were spread out down the mountainside. Pretty ugly. Sad, too.

From where we were standing, I could see the east branch of the Delaware, and the covered bridge with that old elm growing this side of it, so big it nearly obstructed the road. Gray plumes of smoke like feathers on ladies' hats rose up from the chimneys down in Pepacton village.

The sun came flickering through the trees behind us; the sky turned a cold blue with clouds racing over. The wind had picked up and I started to feel chilly again. Guess the wind would blow all day, though it was likely to be the least of my troubles.

Soon enough, a man and a boy, leading a pair of oxen with a sled behind, came walking down from the Sugarloaf Mountain side of the hollow to the south. The man was short with thick arms, a belly like a keg, and a full beard turning white.

When they got to us, Pa said, "This here's . . . my boy . . . Ha . . . Harley."

Harley? What kind of sorry joke was this? I took a step back and pulled a long, frowning, and disbelieving face. Pa glanced over his shoulder at me. I saw the devil wink in his eyes. I gave him a devil of a look right back for not warning me. I had half a mind to kick him, but the other half of my mind said Pa must have a good reason, so I'd best play along like he'd told me to the night before.

Pa took a plug of tobacco and stuck it in his mouth. The other two did the same. The man was Rastus, his son, Jasper.

"Pleased to meet you, son," Rastus said, smiling. His eyes smiled, too. I could tell right off that he was nicer than Pa.

I shied away from his son, only looking sideways at him. I was a girl and he was a real boy all right, a mite shorter than me though. Felt queer about that.

Pa offered me his tin of tobacco. I figured it'd be hateful stuff, but I reckoned it wouldn't go kindly for me to refuse. Figured it'd be a sign of weakness if I did, figured the tobacco wouldn't be as bad as the hell a boy would get if he didn't show himself a man.

I took a pinch and wadded it into the side of my mouth. It was foul, but I managed not to make a face, though a shudder went clear through me. Could've sworn that Pa grinned, enjoying his little prank on me. I'd spit that nasty stuff out first chance I got, which I hoped was pretty quick. Least I knew enough about tobacco not to swallow it or its juice.

Pa told me to work with Jasper, and it wasn't so bad. The oxen had the hardest part, pulling those timbers behind the sled. Pa and Rastus rolled the logs out of the snow with iron hooks. Jasper showed me how to handle the drag shackles, drive the spurs into both sides of a log at one end with mallets. The chains were about ten feet and heavy to handle, too. Glad I'd learned to swing an ax, chopping firewood on the block at home. Before long, I got the right rhythm and swinging a mallet didn't seem to bother my shoulder or arm a'tall. Nobody spoke except to holler orders.

Rastus and Pa hitched the drag chains to the sled, took turns driving the oxen to a steep bank where the logs were skidded down to the edge of the stream.

We broke out our dinner pails when the sun was high overhead. I sat on a low stump; Jasper came and sat nearby. I looked at him good then. He was rugged for sure, but he had a comely face, which made me dislike him right off — black curly hair, long lashes, kind brown eyes like his pa's, warm smooth skin darkened by the sun.

"What's Jasper mean?" I asked, biting into my sandwich. I figured if I asked enough questions, it wouldn't give him room to ask me any.

"Some sort of stone," he said. "What's a Harley?"

"Dumb name, since you're asking," I muttered. Figured Pa started to say Hattie and Harley was the only name that he could think of real quick. Couldn't even take the time to pick me a good name, one from the Bible, maybe, like Daniel or Samuel or Stephen. "Been working in the woods long?"

"Three years."

"How old are you?"

"Almost thirteen. You?"

"Eleven." I took another bite. "You been down the river?"

"Yeah. Lots of times."

"You got any schooling?"

"Some. You?"

"Seventh grade."

Jasper rubbed his chin. "Skipped some grades, huh?"

"Yup." Didn't care to say Ma had taught me. "Figure the teacher was looking to get rid of me," I said.

A smile pulled at the corners of Jasper's mouth. "How come you ain't worked in the woods till now?"

"Maybe Pa didn't need me before." I started to feel cold again.

Jasper chuckled. "Maybe you was just too scrawny before."

"Yup," I said, biting my lip. I'd have to watch my tongue. Schooling or not, Jasper was nobody's fool. Thankfully, Pa and Rastus hollered for us to get back to work. Everybody took time to do their business private, so I had no more worries about that.

We worked steady till the sun started to set across the river. I was tuckered out by that time, wondered how I'd ever get up the mountain again to home. I did, though. Hung my hat next to Pa's on the peg. Pa didn't say a word. Handed me the bottle of liniment, built the fire, and made biscuits better than mine. It just felt like one more sorry joke on me. He knew it, too.

Chapter Five

After supper, Pa sat and whittled hickory pegs and withes for fastening the logs together later on, when it was time to build the rafts. I watched for a while. I always liked to see Pa with his big hands make withes, whittling and shaving pieces of wood into thin strips, bending them like hairpins to loop over the saplings that lashed the logs together.

Before long, I went up to the loft and flung myself down on my mattress. Since there was still some light from Pa's lamp, I took out Ma's diary and scrawled beneath my last entry.

March 15 — Hattie Belle worked like an ox today.

I wrote it the way Ma would, knowing she would've scolded Pa.

Sorry I was mad at you, Ma. I did all right today. I think it'll be okay for a while. Jasper and his pa are real nice. Jasper likes to talk more than I do. That's something.

I was too tired to write more. I pulled the wool blanket over me, fell asleep with the diary still in my hand. Didn't wake up till morning.

I was sore all over; didn't want to move for the hurting. Felt like I could sleep till summer.

"Hey, boy, get your lazy arse out of bed," Pa yelled.

Least he didn't call me Harley. I felt better after I started moving around. By the time we finished our breakfast and started out, I guessed I'd live another day. Wished I could shed being a boy. Didn't know how. Pa was right, I was no cook, and a dead cow didn't need tending. Way I saw it, I was only useful to Pa if I was a boy.

When we got to the logging site, Jasper and his pa were already there. "Hey, Harley, how you faring this fine morning?" Jasper asked, with a good-natured grin, when we reached them.

I just grunted. Everybody laughed. I laughed, too. I sounded just like Pa. Pa took a plug of tobacco and passed me the tin. I grunted again and passed it on to Jasper, and he handed it on to his pa. Guess it didn't matter if a boy chewed or not. That made me real glad.

Later, when we were working, Jasper told me I looked like Pa.

I threw down my mallet. "How in blazes can you tell a thing like that? You can't see his face."

"The eyes. You got your pa's keen blue eyes, same color hair, same way of throwing things, getting all riled up over nothing."

I turned my back to him and kept on working. Didn't want him to see I was crying. Nothing like being a girl and having it told to your face that you're as plug-ugly as your pa, and mean to boot.

I was over it by the time we broke for dinner. Jasper sat with me. I was grateful. I wanted to tell him I was sorry, but figured a boy wouldn't do that unless his ma was twisting his ear to make him. "Hey, Jasper," I said. "Want one of my sandwiches?"

"What you got?"

"Ham."

Jasper nodded. I grinned and handed it over to him. Jasper was what Ma would've called a growing boy. He ate his lunch and half of mine, still eyeing every bite I took like a dog wagging its tail, waiting for a crumb to drop.

Hungry as I was, I still couldn't put away food the way Jasper did.

Jasper set to talking. He talked about hunting game, tracking animals in the woods, fishing, trapping, stuff I'd never done, didn't care to do except for fishing and tracking animals. I stayed intent on my food, mumbling best I could if he asked me a question.

"Harley, you got a rifle?"

I shook my head.

"Darn it all, that ain't right," Jasper said. He looked at Pa, then back at me, leaned forward. "He ever take you hunting, ever teach you to shoot?"

I shook my head again, tried to look very sorrowful.

"That ain't right," he said again. "Tell you what, Harley, after we get these logs down to Philadelphia, I'll take you. I'll teach you. We could do some fishing, too."

"That'd suit me fine, Jasper," I said.

Jasper was quiet for a minute, studying me. "Tell you what, Harley. I can't figure it out. Your pa's got a temper sometimes, doesn't say much, but he just ain't the sort to slight his own boy."

I swallowed real slow, my heart drumming in my ears. Jasper watched me real close as if he expected an answer, a good answer, one that was truthful. I didn't have one. Nothing, not one simple word came to mind.

Jasper sighed like he was disappointed. "Guess you was a sickly child, huh?" he said kindly.

"Won't deny it," I said, which was as close to the truth as I was willing to get.

We hauled ourselves back to work then. Glad of it, too. If he figured out I was no boy, he'd probably hate me. But, for a good time to come, we'd be two boys working side by side. If I was careful, real careful, watched my words before they slipped off my tongue, I'd have me a friend for a while. Jasper was the one and only good reason to put up with being a boy.

Chapter Six

It grew warmer overnight, and by morning the snow was starting to melt. Ma always told me not to trust March. Ma said one day March was warm and inviting, the next bitter and cold.

At breakfast, Pa didn't talk, but his usual frown was replaced by something near like a smile. It was about as cheerful as he ever looked these days. He ate, shoveling his food in without looking up from his plate, and swilled down his coffee while pushing back his chair and getting up from the table.

I'd only eaten a couple of mouthfuls, but I scrambled to get our dinner pails packed with leftover griddlecakes drizzled with honey and some chunks of ham. Pa went striding out the door 'fore I was done. I had to run to catch up to him.

Jasper was all smiles that morning, and just as eager as Pa to get to work. We pushed ourselves hard all right, but the day seemed easier, the chains lighter, our mallets more sure.

When we broke to eat, Jasper explained that once the ice and snow started to melt and the streams ran free, we'd begin building the rafts. "Before you know it, we'll be going down the river," Jasper told me. "Harley, there's nothing more exciting in the world."

They were all excited. Saw Pa jawing to Rastus like a *crakking* crow. Hadn't seen Pa talk that much since before Ma took sick.

"What's a matter with you, Harley?" Jasper said. "Ain't you excited?"

No, I was ruffed up with anger like a grouse. What I wanted to do was scream and kick something. Fine and dandy for them. They were men. It might be a fine high adventure for them, but I was a girl. I wanted my ma and I wanted to wear a dress and I wanted to go back to school again, and I was going to tell Pa. I was not going to go down the river on a raft, nohow.

"Wait till we get to Philadelphia or New York. Pa said we might go to New York this time. He said . . . aw, gee,"

40

Jasper said. He closed his eyes for a second, drew in his breath like he'd slammed a finger with the mallet. He lowered his head; then just took up his excited talk again. "You can't imagine all the people, the streetcars, the carriages, and the stores. Why, there's more stores than trees in that forest over there," Jasper said, waving his arm toward an uncut part of hillside to our west. "What you planning to buy with your earnings?"

"Earnings? Pa didn't say anything about money."

"He will," Jasper said. "Any man or boy who works as a hand on a raft gets paid for it."

"How much? How much will a young hand like me get?"

Jasper shrugged. "Enough for anything you want, I suspect. You could buy yourself a rifle. That way, we could go hunting together."

I coughed, nearly choked. Jasper was thinking about hunting; I was thinking about a dress and a bonnet trimmed with ribbons and lace like the girls in Downsville wore. Even if I was nothing but a Hill Hawk, I still favored wearing a dress instead of these overalls.

Jasper didn't let up. "No need to be scared, Harley," he said, lowering his voice. "That's not to say it can't be dangerous, a mite scary at times, but, mainly, it's just a darn good frolic, more like play than work if you know what you're doing."

Exactly. If you knew what you were doing, but I didn't. Not one bit. I had a bigger worry though, keeping my secret from Jasper. Maybe I should tell him, just blurt out I was a girl and be done with it. But what if he hated me? Didn't want Jasper to hate me, nohow. He was the only friend I'd ever had. Didn't know what to say, so I lied. "I'm thinking you're right, Jasper. I sure could use a rifle." I even rubbed my chin the way men do when they've studied up and clearly calculated a situation.

"You're all right, Harley," Jasper said, when we started back to work. "I knew you'd catch the rafting fever just like the rest of us."

Yup. Just like all the men. When I was swinging that heavy mallet, I thought about Ma, how work seemed to make her weaker. But hauling heavy chains and sweating under the warm March sun just seemed to make me stronger.

Ma never took to life in the hills or, maybe, it was just life that Ma never got comfortable with. She'd never complained, but every so often she'd get a poor spell and I'd find her sitting under her plum tree, staring up at a patch of blue sky, like she was watching, waiting for something, angels, maybe.

"You're sweating like an overworked ox," Jasper said. "You ought to unbutton your underwear like the rest of us."

"Naw," I said.

"What's a matter, you a sissy?" he teased.

"Sissy?" I said. I threw down my mallet and put up my fists. "Want to fight about it?"

Jasper just laughed. "Bet you won't unbutton your shirt 'cause you ain't got any chest hair yet," he said, fingering his straggly few.

"Haw," I said, feeling relieved. Jasper was only funning me. "You'll just have to wonder about that."

Quitting time was pretty late on these warm days, but today, when we packed up to start home, Pa told me to go on ahead. Said he had some business to tend to in Downsville. I figured I knew what business he meant.

"Amos, you should take your boy along," Rastus said. "Do him good to be in town now and then. He's earned it. Hung right in there with us. Don't expect he'll cause you any trouble. Might need him to find your way home."

"Boy's got chores at home," Pa said. He lowered his

voice. "I got private business to see about 'fore the ice breaks, Rastus." Pa turned his back to us. He started walking off down the hillside alone.

Rastus put a hand on my shoulder. "Can't be sure what's on a man's mind. Things aren't always what they seem, son," he said. "Don't you worry none. Your pa's not up to no mischief." But his eyes said he was sorry for something, my pa getting drunk again, maybe.

"Harley, watch yourself going home through the woods," Jasper said.

"Might want to lay in some extra wood tonight, too," Rastus said, sniffing the air. "It's turning damp. Might be rain, might be snow. Hard to tell what we're going to get in March."

I put on my coat and picked up our dinner buckets, watched Jasper and his pa going up the hill away from me. Then I started off in the opposite direction toward home. I wasn't afraid. I minded Pa getting drunk, but I didn't mind the chance to be by myself. It was easy enough to follow our trail through the snow, long as it was still daylight.

By the time I got back to the cabin, it had already gotten cold. Dark clouds were starting to move in from the north. Rastus was right about a storm. The wood box was close to empty, so I filled it, piling it up over the top. By the time I brought in the last armload, it had started to snow.

First the flakes came down soft and pretty the way Ma loved to see them — white feathers falling from angels' wings, she used to tell me. Soon enough the flakes turned to a heavy, driving snow that piled up quickly, covering our tracks and our paths beaten to the barn, to the spring, and into the woods.

Pa had been out many a time in a snowstorm this winter, wading his drunken way home through the woods. Guessed he knew enough to stay in town if the storm was too fierce. I suspected he might not make it home this night. I took his bearskin cap and kicked it into the corner where it belonged.

I sang, happy to have some peace away from Pa, happy to be Hattie again. I put the big pot on the stove and set to making a soup of potatoes and rutabagas, onions and parsnips, carrots and cabbage, and the ham bone. I mixed up dumplings to put over the top when the soup was close to done. Tomorrow I'd make bread enough for a week.

After that, I scrubbed myself good all over, my head, too, and put on my too small dress. Then I fetched Ma's diary from the loft and kept myself company by reading Ma's words aloud and adding some of my own. The fire sizzled, the soup pot simmered with delicious smells, and for that whole sweet, snowy evening, I was Hattie Belle Basket again. I did not give one thought to Pa or his brown whiskey jug.

Chapter Seven

Pa did not come home that night. No sign of him in the morning. I dressed in my long johns and overalls again. Took the shovel and started clearing a path to the barn and the spring. The new snow was deep and wet; clear up above my knees and hard to shovel. The sun was hot in a warm blue sky. The snow settled, melted, became slush and muck in the paths I'd made.

Pa still did not come home.

I swept the hard-packed dirt floor, took a stick and drew some posies in it the way Ma used to, washed the tin plates and cups, filled the wood box again, baked the bread, put the loaves to cool.

Pa still did not come home. I went out to the end of my shoveled path and whistled long and high and shrill like a hawk. But Pa did not whistle back.

When the sun started down the other side of the sky, I set to fretting. Didn't know what to do. Figured Pa might've spent the night in Downsville but he'd have come home by now. Didn't know if I should start out looking for him. Didn't want to think of him getting lost in the storm while I was feeling warm and happy to have him gone for a spell.

Sundown and no sign of Pa. I warmed some soup and dumplings. The stars came out; the moon came up. I was still alone. I got the diary and wrote in the manner of my ma: *Hattie Belle Basket is a wicked girl for hating her pa.* Then I added, *I never wished him a bit of harm, Ma.* Which was true only at the moment I wrote it. Guess I am wicked.

I thought about how Pa used to be, and about the wooden sled he made me for Christmas once that was big enough for the two of us to ride on. Ma wouldn't go, but on snowy days when Pa couldn't work, he'd spend a whole afternoon with me just flying down the hillock to the next rise. We'd pull the sled back up the hill and go down again. It was pretty near as good as rafting, Pa said.

I thought about when Pa went rafting and we would count the days until he got back. If he was gone longer than six days, Ma started to fret. But he always came by the seventh day, loaded down with fresh provisions. If the ice went out early and the river stayed high, Pa would make eight or ten trips down the river. We always knew when he was home to stay, 'cause he'd come in, unload the food supplies, and say, "Hattie Belle, I think something extra fell into my deep pockets this trip for my girls. Why don't you look?"

One pocket was for me and one was for Ma. He brought all sorts of things — violet water and scented sachets and French-milled soaps, toothbrushes, nail brushes, hairbrushes, fancy combs, hairpins, safety pins, shawl pins, linen hankies, buttons, ribbons, real oranges and lemon drops, and clothespins.

One year he brought the diary for Ma. He pulled it out of his inside pocket, said he'd started out with a raft of big logs and the water wore them down so much, there was nothing left but thin sheets of paper. Said he got them bound in leather to give my ma. Even if he didn't talk much, Pa used to have a fun way about everything. But not anymore.

Pa didn't come home that night, either. I set out for work the next day all the same. Picked up the bearskin cap, smoothed the fur, and put it on again. Packed a dinner pail for Pa, too. Figured something must be bad wrong if Pa didn't show.

Pa didn't show. Neither did Jasper or his pa. I whistled, but Pa didn't whistle back. Guess I was the only one dumb enough not to stay put. Didn't know what to do. Sat myself down on a snowy stump till my seat got wet. Didn't know the way to Jasper's or I'd have gone there.

I stared down the mountain at the village. It was a long way down and a longer way back. I had two dinner pails to carry. Didn't know anybody down there either, always staying on the hill, going to the school in the next hollow to the north when Ma wasn't teaching me at home.

No matter. I had to find Pa. I grabbed up the pails and set off toward Pepacton. Before I got there, I'd picked out the general store by the big windows with the writing on them and horses standing in front. There were only a few other buildings and houses sprinkled along the road, including a schoolhouse, a church, and a blacksmith shop.

I walked right into the store, heart thumping like a dog's tail, and moved up to the stove in the middle of the store where a bunch of men herded together like cows. Looked them over. None of them was my pa.

"I need to speak to the proprietor, please," I said loudly.

The men guffawed.

"How may I help you, young man?" a man's voice said from the other side of the store. I didn't catch right off that he was talking to me, till he said it again, louder this time. I turned toward the voice. An old man with one arm was standing behind a long counter. Figured he must've been a soldier in the War of the Rebellion.

I went toward him. If I hadn't been fixed on finding Pa, I'd have had a fine time looking over the satin ribbons and combs, buttons and colorful bolts of calico.

"Please, sir," I said. "My pa went to town on Saturday night, and he never came home. Never came to work today, either." I could feel my chin starting to quiver just like a sissy about to cry.

The men around the stove got quiet. The storekeeper cast me a look of kindness. "What's your pa's name, son?" he asked.

"Amos Basket."

"I know the name. Man never says much."

"That's him all right," I said. "Have you seen him?"

The storekeeper shook his head.

"Might have," one of the men by the stove offered. "What's he look like?"

"Tall, long straggly beard, real blue eyes, scowls a lot."

"Yup, I saw him," the same man offered. "He was at the inn for a while the other night, but he left long 'fore I did." Nobody else knew anything.

"Don't know how we could send out a search party in all this snow," one of the men said. "Could be anywhere."

They were all looking around at each other, trying to figure out what to do, how to help me.

"He's probably curled up somewhere with his jug," the shopkeeper offered. "I'd guess he knows these hills pretty well. Probably found a cave."

The men agreed.

"Better go home to your ma," the shopkeeper said. "Your pa will show up. Don't you worry."

"Obliged," I said. When I opened the door and started out, I heard one of the men say, "Dumb Hill Hawks."

"Ignorant your ownselves," I muttered, and pulled the door shut behind me with a loud crack that made their horses jump. There was no one stirring about. Nothing for me to do but head home the only way I knew, the long way, but I could feel meanness sprouting up in me like a patch of nettles.

I put my head down, crossed the road, and went down the lane to the covered bridge. When I came out the other end, I gave a snowdrift a good, mean kick. At once, a strong hand clamped me by the shoulder.

"Hey, boy, what the hell you doing down here?" A big man turned me around and lifted me off the ground with a meaty paw.

"None of your darn business," I said, sinking my teeth into the man's hand. He tried to shake me off, but I hung on fierce as a wildcat.

"It's your pa."

"Pa?" I let go and looked into the man's face. It took me a minute before I could tell it really was him. Pa had gone and gotten his ugly beard shaved off, and his hair and mustache trimmed all nice. He wasn't such a mangy-looking cur after all. Pretty darn good-looking for a Hill Hawk. Glad it was my pa. Real glad I'd bitten him, too.

"Pa, you look right nice," I said. Figured Pa wouldn't go for any flattery, but I was wrong.

He rubbed his cheek, looked pleased. "You got two dinner pails," Pa said.

"Went looking for you, Pa."

Pa didn't say a word about what he'd been up to, just looked thoughtful. Didn't know what else to say to a man who wouldn't invite any talk. Guess a clean face didn't change my pa any, even if it did make him appear friendlier.

Chapter Eight

Pa was different somehow, more than just his smooth face. Still didn't smile. Didn't talk, either. He seemed sad, thoughtful, maybe, like he was trying to study something out. Wondered if it had something to do with the private business he'd told Rastus about. Me, I didn't dare ask Pa about that.

I was wary. Didn't much trust Pa these days. Watched him like a hooty owl. Figured his surly self must have hibernated like a bear and was bound to wake up, growling worse than before.

We didn't go back to the logging site for several days. I cooked and fetched for Pa. He sat and whittled pegs with that studied look on his face, his chewing tobacco and applejack handy on the table. Now and then he spat a stream of tobacco juice into an old kettle on the floor.

I looked at the wood shavings on the floor, but I was afraid to start up our old game of what Pa's logs might become someday. Ma always said pianos, china cabinets, locks or coaches, and paper for books and sheet music. Pa said masts and sailing ships, wheels and wagons, shingles, staves and barrels, stores and saloons and hotels, boardwalks, and hitching rails. I said schools and houses and churches with steeples, picket fences, tables and chairs, and clothespins for me to make my dolls. But tonight, Pa looked as if there was nothing but drinking and sadness in him, and I held my tongue so I didn't have to be sorry about that, too.

The snow was melting so fast you could hear the sound of water trickling everywhere. Overnight, we went from snow to mud. Deep mud.

It was cloudy and warm the morning we went back to work. Pa and I waded and sloshed through slick mud and gullies of water rushing down the mountainside. Muddy streams poured onto the ice, spread out across the top of the frozen river.

Then it began to rain as powerful hard as it had snowed. The streams became vicious torrents; the gullies spilled over, cutting more gullies. Streams forked down the mountainside like lightning striking at the earth. I feared the ground was going to wash out from under us, slide away to the river.

Jasper was right. I was catching the fever. I shivered with pure joy as I stood there in the rain, spellbound like the others, watching as the water wore down the ice and spread mud and logging debris across the river and onto the flatland. It was like witnessing the holy wrath of God in the days of Noah.

"By the good Lord," Rastus said. "That ice is gonna crack up."

"She's gonna give today," Jasper said.

"Ayah," Pa offered.

We were all fidgety, pacing in the rain and watching that magnificent spectacle below. Couldn't keep still, nohow. Decided we'd better give it up or we'd all catch pneumonia and die the way Luke had.

Rastus invited us to his cabin to sit a spell and deliberate till the rain let up. Pa surprised me by agreeing. That was something.

It wasn't far to Jasper's, a little better than three miles — less, maybe, as the crow flies — up around the mountain and back again into the next hollow. It was so rough going that we couldn't talk any, not with the wind and rain beating on us.

Except for the top, Sugarloaf Mountain was mostly logged off; the hollow was bare of trees except for a few straggling near their cabin. They had a nice farm, too — a real barn, several sheds, chicken coop, a fenced-in pasture, small orchard, a fair-sized garden spot, and a field for corn, probably. They'd built on the back of the cabin, put in windows, added a porch. Inside were rooms and a wood floor with colorful braid rugs.

Jasper's mother and sisters, three of them, were rolling out cookie dough and cutting gingerbread men. One of the girls looked to be not much younger than me, though she was shorter and not so scrawny. She had a thick chestnut braid hanging way down her back. She and the littlest one were poking raisins into the dough for eyes. The girls were all wearing wool dresses dyed a pretty shade of elderberry.

The warm smell of molasses and spices filled the cabin. The smell made me miss Ma something fierce. I wanted to cut out cookies, too, the way I used to with Ma, and have Pa come bursting in, joking about how the bears followed him home, all of them smelling our good ginger-and-molasses cookies clear the other side of the hill. He'd pick up a cookie, and then grab a few more, for the bears, he always said. If Jasper's sisters had known I was a girl, I bet they would've let me help.

The way I saw it, Jasper was a lucky dog. I pretty near hated him for having all this when all I had now was Pa.

Jasper's older sister was dainty and she wore her dark hair coiled around her head in a braid same as Ma's, except Ma's was a halo of gold. The girl smiled when she caught me staring at her. Thought I was admiring her like a boy would, I guess. I wasn't. I was wondering what it'd be like to have folk look at you and think you were just plain pretty instead of just plain. I wanted to hear Ma tell me I'd be pretty someday, and for Pa to say I was his girl, not just remember them saying it. Sometimes, it seemed as if I'd made it all up to please myself.

When Rastus began to talk about getting out of the logging business, I momentarily lost interest in the girls. Rastus told my pa he was tired of them working independent. You got to see it yourself, Amos, Rastus told him. Our woods is gone; can't get milk from a dead cow. I giggled into my hand when he said that.

Rastus said it might be his last year to log, thought he might work some for one of the mills and expand his farm. Better for his family, he said. It was clear to me

Rastus already had his mind made up; there wasn't any might or maybe about it.

Jasper was quiet, his face troubled for once like this was the first he'd heard of it. I suspected his pa quitting wouldn't keep him off the river, nohow.

Guess Pa didn't like what Rastus had to say, either. All at once, his face clouded up. "You're going to quit on me, ain't you?" Pa said.

"You know it ain't like that, Amos," Rastus said. "You know a man don't always have a choice about things. You know that, don't you, Amos?"

"Ayah," Pa said, lowering his head like a beaten dog. He didn't say another word. He just got up from the table and strode out of the cabin.

Nothing for me to do but follow. Jasper's sister, the one about my age, pushed a warm gingerbread man into my hands before I got out the door and gave me a look of pity. I wanted to throw that cookie at her and yell that I did not need any of their charity. But I didn't. I lowered my head and tucked that cookie in my pocket to protect it from the rain. I knew it'd break apart, but I wanted that cookie more than I wanted my pride.

One thing I can say about Pa's dark mood, it made me forget my silly notions of waiting to be pretty. I was more particular concerned now with going through the rest of the day without getting cuffed like a bear cub.

Lucky for me, the ice broke up when we were about halfway home. We could hear the thunder and crack of it, the boom echoing across the valley. Pa turned in his tracks and rushed toward the river. I did my best to keep up, splashing and slipping, getting covered in mud, falling down a couple of times. Stood next to Pa on a steep bank and watched that mighty wrathful river roaring through the valley.

"Yahoo!" Pa hollered, tossing his cap into the air. It was something to see, my pa and the river.

I guess the ice going out marked the beginning of something good for Pa. Didn't know what it meant for me. I watched the big chunks of ice breaking up and being swept down the river and wondered what that angry river held in store for me. One thing I knew for sure, that river was not going to erase my longing to be a girl again, especially now that I had a vision stuck in my head of how fine it could be.

PART III

The River

Chapter Nine

After the ice went out, we had to wait again. This time we watched the flooded river like circling hawks, waiting for the streams to quiet enough to begin building the rafts.

The morning we started building the colts, Jasper chattered like a red squirrel. Colts were as long as a raft but half as wide, Jasper told me. He said we had to make them skinny to fit through the narrow places in our branch of the river. He just went on from there and talked about everything.

After a while, a curious smile twitched at Pa's lips. "Best save your breath for working, Jasper," Pa said, in a way that sounded more jovial than gruff.

Rastus grinned. Nodded his agreement. "You can show off later on, son," he said.

Jasper got red-faced and shut up. He saved his talking for eating time when he and I moved off by ourselves. I was eager to learn more about Jasper's sisters, but he looked disgusted when I asked about them. I was thinking how pretty those wool dresses dyed with elderberry were and about the warm smell of gingerbread. But that was girl talk.

"You ever seen my pa in a real fight?" I asked.

Jasper snorted. "He's got a dyed-in-the-wool reputation for it. Everybody wants to fight him 'cause nobody can beat him. He's tough. He's good at fighting just like he is at steering a raft." Jasper relented some, softened his tone for me, maybe. "Well . . . pretty near all the river men love a fight. It can get downright rough even for boys."

"What do boys fight over?" I asked in alarm.

Jasper scowled. "What boys always fight about. You're a boy, ain't you? What do you think?"

"Bigger, faster, better?" I said with a gulp.

"That's the starting place usually," Jasper said. He laughed. "Just don't be too quick to let on to a boy that you're bigger, faster, better, or you'll have to fight for sure. Course, you're pretty young for a rafter, young enough to be left alone. Don't have to worry none; we'll all watch out for you."

I leapt off that log and swung around to face Jasper. "Don't have to fight for me. I'm strong. I can fight for myself," I said putting up my fists.

"Sure, you can." Jasper laughed. "You don't even know how to make a fist; you ain't standing right, and you're leaving yourself wide open to get slugged in the face."

I gulped again. Scowled hard, too. Put my arms down, stuck my hands behind my back.

"Don't get riled," Jasper said. "Look . . . square up your fingers like this," he said, making his hands into fists.

I tried it. That's when Jasper put a hand on one of mine, moved my thumb so it didn't stick out like a handle on a pot. His hand was warm and rugged. "Got awful slender fingers, bones like a . . . a baby bird's." He dropped my hand and backed away. "Best thing is to keep your eyes down if you think trouble's brewing. Somebody looking for a fight will twist your words, no matter what you say. I mean it, Harley. Could be nasty for all of us, your pa especially, if you don't watch yourself."

Our work became more fevered as the river started to simmer down. Every second counted. Mainly, now, I was Pa's fetch boy, but I didn't mind so much, 'cause Jasper was doing the same for his pa. I paid real close attention, watching my pa roll timber into the sheltered cove they'd picked to build the raft.

Pa was good all right. He could stand on a single log, drill holes with an auger, pound in a peg faster than anything. I figured walking on water might be easier.

I can't rightly say why it pleased me so much, but Jasper's pa wasn't near as agile or skilled as mine. I had a powerful urge to gloat even though I supposed it was evident to Jasper that my pa was better. Ma wouldn't approve of me throwing it up to him though. She'd say it wasn't proper to suggest such a thing. Ma was a lady, no doubt about that, but I was not. I was hardly even a girl these days, and I didn't always mind my manners. I was just real glad that I finally had something to brag about.

My mean streak got the better of me after I watched Pa lashing logs together all day, securing them with sapling poles. Pa took a withe, looped it over the lash pole, pounded a peg into the auger hole in the log on both sides to make the raft strong. Pa said he used one long timber, then a shorter one to make sure the joints didn't meet up. Pa said the first part of making a safe journey was building a strong raft.

"Like Noah's ark?" I asked.

"Ayah," Pa said with a chuckle. "Except for the varmints."

I chuckled, too. Funny how Pa could talk right along while he was working on the water. That was something. I watched him, learned there was a rhythm to being on a log that was buffeted by the water, same as there was to swinging a mallet. Pa must have been a real fine dancer like Ma said.

When we quit for the day, I sidled up to Jasper just like that evil old snake in the Garden of Eden did to Eve. "Jasper," I said, whispering poison in his ear. "My pa might be good at fighting, but he's even better at walking on water, lots better than your pa."

Jasper swung around and gave me the blackest look ever. "You better watch your mouth, Harley, or the first boy you'll be fighting is me, and you know you can't beat me."

I just grinned, well . . . sneered, to be exact. "Can so."

Guess Jasper didn't know what to think. He shook his head, backed away from me, didn't even put up his fists.

"You don't know anything, do you, Harley? You don't even know why your pa's taking you along," he said. Then he turned and hustled to catch up to his pa. He didn't look back.

I watched him walk away. Part of me was sorry for being so mean; part of me wasn't. Maybe I didn't know much about fighting, but one thing I knew for sure — I was a girl, but I was no chicken.

Chapter Ten

That night, I burned the biscuits on the bottom and the gravy was thick as paste and I let the pot of potatoes scorch. Didn't feel much like looking up from my plate or talking any. I did all the same.

"Ma told me you were a fine dancer," I said.

"She did, did she?" Pa said. He didn't sound mad.

I looked at him from the corner of my eye. He wasn't eating much, just sort of pushing the food around. Best to keep my words few.

"Know what she meant by that after today."

"That so?" Pa sounded interested now.

"Thought you could walk on water if you had a mind to." I looked at Pa this time. He didn't say anything, but he looked back at me like he was inviting me to say more. I warmed to my subject. "Yup," I said. "That's what I told Jasper all right. Told him I could beat him in a fight, too."

"You told him what?" Pa's face went from inviting to troubled just like March. "You tell him anything else?"

"Didn't tell him I was a girl."

Pa still looked troubled. "He say anything about our trip?"

I gulped. I thought about Jasper saying I didn't even know why Pa was taking me along. I swallowed those words and didn't look at Pa. "Jasper said lots of things. How am I supposed to remember them all?"

"Shouldn't go bragging," Pa said. "You're inviting grief when you do." Before I knew what was happening, Pa reached over and cuffed me aside the head, not hard, but my eyes teared up all the same. Cuffing me that way made me hate him enough to be sorry into next year for bragging on him even once.

"Ain't hungry for burned biscuits," he said. He pushed back his plate and stood up.

Then I hated him some more for saying that, even though it was true. I sat stiff and held my breath, afraid he might cuff me again. Guess once was good enough. He grabbed his coat off the peg and went out. I spent the whole night hating so hard, I figured there was nothing left inside of me but solid blackness.

I looked at Pa's plate full of food, and out of spite, to myself, I guess, I choked down every bit of my awful cooking. Pa didn't come back inside, and I did not go look for him. He was either out in the barn with his jug or on his way to the tavern in Pepacton. I took out Ma's diary.

Dear Ma,

Till tonight, I was getting to be as mean as Pa. Now I'm meaner. I'm so mean that I'm starting to hate myself more than I hate Pa. I'm scared I'm going to forget how to be a real girl, and I'm scared that the only thing good inside of me is what I can recollect about you. What can I do, Ma? What makes me so mean to a real nice boy like Jasper? Please don't send me any signs like before. Don't think I could tolerate any at the moment.

I heard Pa come stomping in that night, thunking his jug down on the table and knocking into stuff. I didn't move even a little toe, didn't breathe hardly till I heard him snoring. Hoped I wouldn't have to pester him awake in the morning.

The next morning, I found a box of food on the

table — ham, big hunk of cheese, salt pork, cans of beans and corned beef, a sack of flour, eggs, jug of milk, and a hat, one with a wide brim like Pa wore for rafting. I was afraid to touch any of it.

Pa got up right after I started fixing the fire. He hardly looked bleary-eyed at all. Wasn't surly, either, even talked some during breakfast. Pa told me to stay home and make some decent bread, enough to last several days, some pandowdy or cookies. He'd like a plum pie, apple would do. Guessed he'd have to content himself with watching the other men eat theirs. I knew my pie dough was tough and tasteless. Neither it nor I got along with the rolling pin. Pie was a useless undertaking for me.

"Get yourself good and ready, 'cause tomorrow we're shoving off," Pa said, when he was pulling on his cap, ready to go out the door. "The hat's for you," he added, as he stepped outside.

I watched him from the open doorway, saw him stop by Ma's plum tree and take off his cap, bow his head. I got a lump in my throat and moved back out of sight. Guess Pa's wound was festering as much as my own. Guess what we both needed was a powerful dose of Ma to sweeten us up again.

Chapter Eleven

Next morning, Pa woke me. Startled me, too, poking his head up, looking at me in the loft. "Hey, there, it's time to get going," he called softly, excitedly, the way he used to on Christmas morning.

Outside, it was still black as my burned biscuits, but I got right up, pulled on my overalls. I could hear thumping below, so I peeked over the edge of the loft. Pa was pretty near dancing a jig while he flipped the griddle-cakes. Guess today was better than Christmas for Pa. He'd even shaved his face clean again, except for his mustache. He hadn't acted this lively since before Ma died. It was a good beginning for our trip.

Before going down, I thought to stick Ma's diary inside my shirt. Didn't know if I'd have time to write, but at least I'd have this little bit of Ma with me. When Pa wasn't looking, I'd shove it in the deep inner pocket of my overcoat.

Pa had breakfast spread on the table and a mug of hot coffee poured for me. The dinner box for our noon meals was packed up and sitting by the door. Pa had done everything.

We wolfed down our breakfast, pushed back our chairs, and headed out, leaving our plates on the table like we'd be back home that night. That was strange, too. I'd never been away from home overnight. Never been anywhere but Pepacton and once to Downsville for a medicine show.

I don't know what came over me when I thought about going clear to Philadelphia or maybe New York like Jasper said, but for once, I didn't mind dressing the part of a boy, because I was going away from the mountain, going to see some of the world. Jasper thought rafting was a frolic; Pa said it was like riding down a long hill on a sled. Figured I could stand a little fun myself. Jasper had told me plenty about the cities, too — the people, horses and carriages, hansom cabs, trolley cars, trains, and the noise, the smells and the stores. But all I could picture in my mind was Kingston and Ma's stories about growing up in a big house with walking paths, flower gardens and flowering trees, and a green lawn where she played croquet or sipped lemonade and read Longfellow's poetry in the shade.

The moon was getting ready to set, and the sky was still scattered over with pale stars when we left the cabin. It'd gotten plenty cold: the ground sparkled with frost; tree branches shimmered; the mud, turned solid overnight, was embedded with crystals of ice. Our breath made puffs of fog in front of us. There was no wind.

Pa and I walked along, carrying the food hamper between us. I didn't mind the early morning quiet for once. The riot of work would start soon enough.

When we got to the river, Jasper and his pa hadn't arrived. The colts were built and safely anchored with ropes to tree stumps near the shore. Pa leapt onto the first raft and I leapt after him. Soon as I landed, I fell. Didn't know it'd be like leaping on the back of something alive and running. "Not much like riding a sled, Pa," I said.

Pa laughed and gave me a hand up. "You wait; you'll get your river legs by the time Jasper shows up, I s'pect," he said.

I helped Pa load the hamper, tie it down with a rope to

a lashing pole in the center of the raft. Far as I could tell, that hamper was going to be the only place to sit without getting a wet seat.

"Let's get you some practice," Pa said. "We'll pace off the length and width of the raft, see exactly how much timber we got." Pa put one foot in front of the other. "One of my boots is close enough to one foot," he said. "You walk along next to me and count my steps out loud."

Pa was smart about that all right. I got to concentrating on my counting and forgot about my shaky legs. End to end our little colt was two hundred and twenty footsteps long, side to side it was only twenty-four steps.

"How many steps to cross the river, Pa?" I asked.

Pa glanced from shore to shore, smoothed his mustache some. "Quite a few. More than I can calculate right offhand. How many would you say?"

I looked across and back again, rubbed my cheek. "Yup. Quite a few," I said.

Pa grinned. "This here's just one branch on a mighty big tree. Wait till we get farther down, when you get to see the trunk. Like the bottom of a tree trunk, the river gets wider as we go along. Never had time to measure out the distance."

After that, Pa showed me my oar. It was a giant — six times longer than I was tall, the blade alone made three of me. The oar was fastened with pins that Pa called locks to an oak block that was centered at the front of the raft.

"Here, try it out," Pa said.

I put my hands around the narrow stem of the oar. "Fits my hand just right, Pa," I said in surprise.

"Made it special, so you could get a good grip," he said.

"That was right thoughtful of you, Pa," I said.

"Ayah." Pa turned away and spit a stream of tobacco juice over the side. Guess he didn't want any more said about that.

One good thing, once I took up my oar, I was standing a good ways back from the bow, pretty near twelve feet by my rough calculations. Glad I could stand away from the rushing current.

Pa showed me how to work my oar. "Heck of a lot easier than it looks," Pa said. "See, pulling an oar is not the same as paddling. You don't dip deep. Just swivel the oar left and right, up and down in those oarlocks. When I say pull, it's never to move the raft forward — the river takes care of that — but to push it left or right toward or away from the shores or rock ledges or boulders or bridge piers."

He was calm as the water in the eddy where the rafts were tied up. He went over everything real slow and careful, walking alongside of me as I tried out the oar. The water lapped at the raft all around us, and splashed up between the timbers.

"That sound remind you of anything?" Pa asked.

I listened to the water. Had no idea what he was talking about. I listened some more. "Like swinging an ax," I blurted out.

Pa looked pleased. "Yup," he said. "Keep that sound and rhythm stuck in your head like a song. Think of the movement of water as breath and wind. Breathing with the river is like being a hawk knowing when to ride a current of air and when to flap its wings. Not much work to it when you know how. Never saw a hawk crash into trees or the sides of mountains, either. They fly alert and watchful. We got to do the same."

I got a clear picture in my head of what Pa meant about the hawks, but I wasn't sure I understood, exactly, what that meant for me.

Pa went on, "I'm the pilot, the river perils belong to me. All you have to do is act lively when I holler a command. I stand at the rear on the Pennsylvania side, and if I holler 'Pennsylvania,' you pull to the right with your oar. If I holler 'Jersey,' you pull to the left. If I want you to change quick, I'll holler 'Holt, t'other way.' If I don't want you to pull with the oar, I'll yell 'Holt.' That's about it for now."

By that time, the sun was coming up. Shortly after, Jasper and his pa arrived like it was a real holiday, with a horse and wagon and all their womenfolk on board to see them off. The girls were wearing wool capes and matching bonnets of evening blue, their cheeks a rosy blush from the morning cold. They waved and called out a greeting to me — Harley. They chattered and quarreled with each other in a friendly way and bustled with the food hampers for their pa and brother.

The girl about my age came over to Pa and me. She was carrying a basket on one arm. The closer she got, the shabbier and plainer I felt. She held the basket out to me. "We made you and your pa an apple pie for the trip, and crullers fried fresh this very morning," she said. "I'm Edith." She stood at the edge of the cove next to our raft.

Pa leaned over and lifted the basket from her out-stretched hand. "Thankee, miss. Much obliged," he said, tipping his hat to her.

I didn't know if I was more dumbstruck by Pa's mannerly actions or Edith batting her eyes at me. The latter made me feel more than a mite uneasy.

"Looks like you got yourself an admirer, Harley," Jasper called out cheerfully.

Edith turned her head and stuck her nose in the air. "I was just being neighborly, Jasper," she said.

"Yup," Jasper said, fluttering his eyelids at her.

"Bye, Harley," she said, swishing her skirts as she started back to her mama.

"Bye, Harley," Jasper said in a high voice.

I didn't say a word.

"Cat got your tongue, huh?" Pa said with a chuckle.

"What's the matter, Harley?" Jasper called from the adjoining raft. "Ain't a girl ever flirted with you before?"

"Nope. I was a sickly child, remember. Girls don't favor sickly boys."

Jasper laughed, came over to the edge of his colt, and leapt across to me. "You ain't sickly now. You got pretty big muscles, even if you ain't got much of an Adam's apple yet."

Why would he go noticing a thing like that? His Adam's apple wasn't much to brag on.

"Maybe, that's because I get lots more practice eating

my words than you," I said boldly. All the same, I sucked in my breath and held it, scared of what he might come out with next.

Jasper grinned and slapped his thigh. "Maybe I was wrong about you, Harley. Guess you can take a joke after all."

"Sure I can," I said, grinning back. Glad he was teasing. Still, he was getting a mite too curious about my looks. Guess that was part of what Pa was trying to tell me about being alert and watchful like a hawk, and not bragging about stuff.

"Come on, boys, man your oars," Pa said, still in a fair mood. "It's time for us to be shoving off!"

Chapter Twelve

Pa untied the raft and we pushed off with long poles and slid away from the shore and out of the protected cove. As soon as the bow came out of the eddy, we were carried into the rushing current of the river. It was thrilling. I felt like a young bird using my wings for the first time, soaring and dipping, my heart beating happiness, and the wind playing sweetly along.

Jasper and his pa came out right behind us. Jasper's sisters and their ma made a pretty sight lined up in a row along the bank like blue jays on a tree branch.

"Goodbye, Pa. Goodbye, Jasper!" they shrieked happily. Then, in a lull, Edith called, "Bye, Harley." I swear her voice echoed up and down the valley. I was facing the shore, because of the way I was pulling the oar toward the Pennsylvania side. Nothing for me to do but give her a little wave, which made all the girls shriek. Didn't know a gaggle of girls could be so silly. I'd never acted that way.

Didn't know who to feel sorrier for though, me or poor Edith, who thought I was a boy. Wouldn't mind having her for a friend, maybe. But would they want to be friends with me if they learned the truth? Would Jasper? I looked at him smiling and pulling easy on his oar, and I got a lump in my throat. Didn't want to lose Jasper as a friend, nohow. Didn't want to be a boy, either. I was stuck, no doubt about it.

Jasper's family stayed on the bank and waved until we were out of sight just like we were something special, soldiers going off to war, maybe.

Our colt was first, because Pa was the best pilot, and I knew he was watchful and alert with keen eyes. I felt important, being the one to stand at the front of our fleet. I thought it must really be like flying, the way we rushed along in the swollen river. I wondered if young hawks were ever afraid the way I was now. I wondered if the breath of the sky felt the same under their wings as the breath of the river felt rushing beneath my feet. Wondered if they feared falling or getting blown off course by a sudden wild gust.

It was scary to be standing at the front with my back to the bow, not seeing where we were going, keeping a steady eye on Pa, but I was flying, soaring like a red-tailed hawk in the sky. That was really something.

After those first jittery moments, I liked the feel of the river, its restless voice singing a song of its own as it pushed us along. I wanted to turn and face downriver though, especially when I heard the crowd cheering from the banks before we even got to the covered bridge in Downsville.

As we floated past, I saw the townsfolk lined up on the banks, dressed in their good clothes like it was a holiday. Women waved white hankies, but the boys, some of the girls, too, ran along the bank and tried to keep up with us. They waved, called out to us, wished us a safe journey and Godspeed. I waved back real hard, smiled big. Guess I didn't look much like a seasoned rafter. Didn't care. That was something special to have all those folk come out to see us off and wish us well.

Along the way, in every eddy and inlet and every saw-mill, more rafts were pushing off or being built, and more colts were coming up behind us from the towns above — Arena, Shavertown, Union Grove. Before we went around the horseshoe bend below Downsville, I could see ten, maybe twelve more colts coming down the river, spread out in a line like a skein of geese.

Made me wonder why Ma and I had never come. Pa would've liked that probably, having us come down to the river to see him off. Ma never liked to be seen much, though, thought folk talked about her. She was right about that. She told me once that she didn't belong, wasn't like the people here. Sometimes I thought she was ashamed, not of Pa, exactly, but of being thought a Hill Hawk herself. Wished Ma could see the crowd today. Guess she'd see that we both missed out on a lot of good times.

It was hard to keep watching Pa, but when he hollered "Holt t'other way," I got to turn and walk toward the opposite side of the raft. Then I could see what was going on in front of me. Back and forth I went, pulling the oar toward the Pennsylvania side then over to the Jersey side whenever Pa said. Sometimes I swear I knew when to turn before Pa hollered by the tugging of the water on the raft, pulling us toward one shore or the other and out of the main channel.

More rafts came into view the farther downriver we went. Seemed as if it wouldn't be too much trouble to walk from raft to raft the whole way to Philadelphia.

Some of the colts were loaded with sawed lumber, barrels and kegs, or other goods, but ours were just the logs themselves. Pa and Rastus would sell our logs to a mill. I hoped our logs would be made into paper for something special like books and sheet music. Ma would like that.

Pa called out to some of the men still building rafts along the shore as we passed by. He hollered out the names of some of the hamlets and islands, eddies and brooks, so I knew what they were. Just past Tater Island, we came up on Vernold's Eddy, where a man about Pa's size, only heavier built and with a peg leg, was laying the cribbing on his colt.

"Howdy, Lew," Pa hailed in a jolly voice.

"Take the Jersey channel at the twist, Amos. Raft stove up on t'other side." He called over, cupping both his hands around his mouth.

Pa gave him a thumbs-up and a broad grin. "Pull Jersey," Pa hollered, as soon as we got to the bend in the river.

It was a hard pull to the left, but when I switched to the Jersey side, I saw the raft Lew had told Pa to watch for, run aground on Enoch Island. Nobody was hurt, I guess, but a couple of the logs had broken free from the lash poles on the right side of the bow where it was run aground. The tail end stuck out across the channel. Men were hustling to secure the logs with the lash poles again.

It was tight going down through the narrow channel to the left of the island. We slid a little on the shore rocks, scraped off some of the bark, took some of the muddy bank along. But it was easy enough going. My legs were steady now, my arms strong and sure as I pulled on the oar. I learned quick enough to raise the oar just enough to clear the water and pull again. Jasper was right — rafting was a frolic.

We passed through Elk Rift and Ham's Gut and on to Shinhopple, where some men were putting a big raft into the water. Pa hollered, "Hey, Eb. Hey, Rollie," as we went by. They waved and hailed us back.

By this time, the sun was up, glowing warmth over the frosty morning. The thawing smell of spring was in the air. I was feeling bright as the day to be out here in the world, going someplace, instead of staying alone in a little cabin surrounded by darkness and mud. Maybe there were only men and boys out here, but it wasn't bad. When Pa hollered out, "Pull," I wasn't the only one pulling. It was as if every one of us riding these river rafts were pulling together.

The morning slipped by as quickly as our colt did over

the whorling, breathing river. We pushed on past the village of East Branch, where the Beaverkill rushed in from the east and joined our Pepacton. We pulled our rafts up at the next village, Fish's Eddy. The river was wider now, wide enough to lash the colts together.

My legs trembled when I stepped back on the ground. I tottered a bit when I walked. Couldn't get over the feeling that I was still moving. Felt a bit dizzy for a minute, too.

Pa and Rastus set to putting our two rafts together, working at a breakneck speed. After that, we got the dinner pails out of the hampers, and just like every day in the woods, I ate with Jasper.

"How did you like it, Harley?" Jasper asked.

"Liked it fine. Felt like a bird soaring over the world," I said, spreading my arms like wings.

Jasper laughed. "You did fine, too," he said. "When I got a second to look, I thought you was having a real good time."

"I was, Jasper. Better than I ever thought, I'll tell you that."

"First time I went out," Jasper said, dropping his voice some, "I pulled the wrong way back there at Enoch Island. Pulled us right into the shore."

"You get hurt any? Did the colt break?"

"Naw," Jasper said. "Only thing that got hurt any was my feelings. My pa just laughed, yours, too. But you're a natural, Harley, just like your pa."

I felt good about that, important.

Plenty of the men who put to shore here to lash their colts together stopped to jaw about the good day for rafting. Most of them knew Pa, wanted to be introduced to his son. They had an encouraging word for me. Had stories of their first trips when they were young shavers like Jasper and me. Slapped me on the back, told me I must be pretty darn good to get this far without running aground.

Guess I was feeling pretty pleased with myself and talking proud about how I pulled us right around those islands like it was nothing. I didn't miss Pa's scowl, no sir, but I couldn't stop smiling and joking with the men. I felt good all right, and for once I was not going to worry about being a girl or about my pa getting riled if I chattered like a chipmunk.

Chapter Thirteen

Pa pulled me aside after we had packed up our dinner hampers and secured the tools on the raft. He held tight to my arm, lowered his voice, glared down at me. "Running the river is risky business. You best get that chip off your shoulder, 'fore something comes along and knocks it off for you."

I knew it was mean of me, because I was glorying in being on this river trip, but I spat out anyway, "Guess I'm nothing but a chip off the old block." I yanked my arm away, walked to the other end of the raft, and took my place near Jasper. Pa let me go. Didn't say another word, didn't cuff me for acting big, either. Guess he knew I was right.

"Hey, Jasper," I said.

Jasper shook his head, scuffled his feet on the cribbing. "Shouldn't talk to your pa that way, Harley. He's right, you know."

"Thought you were on my side."

"I am. Your pa's tough, got a temper that'll burn up a mountain, but it still ain't right for you to disrespect him."

"Why shouldn't I? He's not particular fond of me, Jasper."

"Sure he is. You don't see it, that's all."

"Don't see it, 'cause it isn't there."

Jasper scowled. "There's plenty you don't see, plenty you don't know, either," he muttered.

"Might be you're the one who doesn't know everything," I said, forgetting myself.

"I swear, Harley, sometimes you're as spiteful as a girl," Jasper said.

That shut my mouth.

"Stop that jawing," Pa hollered. "We got us a job to do."

We pushed off then, back into the current, this time with a mighty big raft, forty-eight feet wide and longer than the covered bridge across the river in Pepacton.

The river was smooth for a ways, running wild but with no rocks jutting up or rifts of white water. We'd gone a few miles, I guess, when Jasper called over. "Brace yourself, Harley. We're coming to some rapids."

"Pease Island," Pa hollered. "Pull Pennsylvania. Pull hard. All hands pull."

Already, I knew to hate islands. We moved into the channel on the Pennsylvania side, but, sweet as you please, Pa steered us around the sharp bend in the narrows by Hawk's Point, the water frothing over the bow, soaking me and Jasper with spray.

After that, the valley widened out. We were nearly to Hancock, Jasper told me.

We were slipping along through the middle of the town, slick as anything, having us a pretty calm ride, too, calm enough for Pa and Rastus to pass the jug a couple of times. We were coming up to a bridge when a loud noise pierced the air, then again, over and over. I looked around, saw the train come chugging around a bend, smoke and sparks billowing out of its stack, heard the wheels clacking and rolling, whistle whining like an unearthly monster. Just as we got beneath the trestle, the train barreled across overhead.

I yelped good, let go my oar, dropped belly down on the deck, put my hands over my ears, and squinched my eyes shut. Expected we'd all be killed. Expected that train to come toppling down on top of us.

Don't rightly know how long I lay there, but after a while the deafening sound of the train faded. Then all I heard was laughter.

"Man your oar," Pa hollered. "But leave that chip right where it fell."

I got to my feet, soaked to the skin, wet from the water lapping up through the spaces between the logs, took my place again with a face hot from more than just the sun. I was peeved at Pa for being right. Peeved at my ownself for proving it to him so quick. I knew about trains, but no one ever said that seeing one coming was like watching a black cloud race toward you, making more noise than thunder.

We were still in Hancock, and Jasper got to story-telling. Told me there was a man who owned the American Hotel over there along the railroad tracks whose daughter never came out of her room.

"How come?" I asked.

"Well, it was like this," Jasper said. "She was his only daughter. She was a beauty and could sing like a canary, I'm told."

Pa hollered "Jersey," so we had to turn, but Jasper kept talking over his shoulder.

"So what happened?"

"She fell in love with this officer, a lieutenant in the army during the War of the Rebellion."

"He got killed?"

"No."

"He found another love?"

"No, her father forbade her to see him or even say farewell. He said the officer was not a worthy match for his daughter. After that, she took to her room and has never come out. Now, that's what I call a hateful pa."

I got what he meant all right, but I wouldn't give him the satisfaction of letting on. "What's her name?" I asked.

"Fannie Read."

Poor Fannie Read. I was going to write about her in Ma's diary. Wished I could tell Ma about her for real. In some ways, Ma was like Fannie, keeping herself shut off from the world, not ever wanting to mix with folk. But Ma was different, too. She hadn't let her ma or pa keep her away from her true love.

Guess I wasn't like Ma or Fannie. I was no recluse, and I was not going to let my pa force these poor boy's threads on me forever.

Chapter Fourteen

After we passed through the village of Hancock, New York, Pa hollered for me to cross over and trade places with Jasper. I smarted over that, but not for long. The west branch of the river came tumbling into sight on the Pennsylvania side, tried to push the east branch out of its way.

The force of the two branches coming together was more like a fistfight between schoolboys than the wedding of waters that Pa always called it. The raft was pulled into the midst, Pa shouting the whole time. It wasn't just the waters joining together that caused the clash but the struggle to keep our raft from colliding with a fleet of other rafts speeding down the channel of the west branch, ready to come shooting out into the river at the same time we did. Didn't know how Pa could keep his wits about him and steer our craft out of harm's way. "Pull Jersey," he shouted. "Pull hard to the shore."

We were headed fast toward the rocky shoreline, pushed by the swirling wake of the oncoming fleet. One side or the other, we were going to smash something.

"Holt t'other way," Pa called.

I turned quick and pulled with all my might to get us back to the Pennsylvania side. And there we were smack in the middle of the mighty Delaware, strong and swift and wondrous to behold, that long fleet flying on ahead of us. Pa had saved our hides, no doubt about it!

Couldn't help myself; I nearly wept. A thrill passed through me so exhilarating that I shouted, "Yahoo!" before I could catch myself. Jasper answered me back with a gleeful shout of his own. Pa and Rastus hollered out, too, their shouts punctuated with hefty swigs on the jug.

Myself, I couldn't recall ever feeling so good or so free. Felt like a whole lot of my meanness washed away. Thought I'd burst with pride over Pa. He sure was something on the water. Wished Ma could see for her ownself that being a Hawk was a good thing, something to be proud of.

We moved along swiftly and smoothly for several

miles. Pa said we could rest, sit down on our oars for a bit. The Erie Railroad followed the river on the flat lands spreading out to the left on the New York side. On the Pennsylvania side, the mountains seemed to rise right up out of the water.

At Stockport, the valley and the village sprawled out on both shores with an island farm in between and sawmills where rafts were being built. The ride was smooth, the river winding only a little till we got to Equinunk. The river made a hairpin over to Lordville, and again by the little village of Boucheux.

Jasper said that we should be stopping for the night soon, but Pa gave no sign of letting up. Jasper said rafting usually went from dawn to dark, but Pa loved the thrill of piloting on a clear, moonlit night.

We glided along by a steep mountain with ledges and rock slides and uncut evergreens. "Lots of rattlers in these parts," Jasper said.

I gulped. Looked around over both shoulders. We didn't have rattlesnakes up in Pepacton. At least Pa said no rattlers had ever been seen that far upriver. "Don't see any rattlers," I said.

"Plenty all around through here," Jasper said. "See those rock ledges? There's probably hundreds of the rascals up there. I heard tell that more than seventy rattlers were killed one spring just from one den."

I looked closer at the ledges to see if anything was slithering around. There were suspicious-looking vines and scrubby bunches of gnarled rhododendron that made me shiver.

"Might be some rattlers sunning themselves. They like to do that. They swim across the river sometimes, too. Yup. Lots of rattlers in these parts," Jasper said. "Watch out for rattly tails sticking up out of the water." Jasper stuck up a finger, waggled it, and made a buzzing noise.

"Is that what the rattlers sound like?" I listened, but all I could hear was the rush of water.

"Aw," Jasper said. "Don't know. Seen them drop off the ledges, though, like they was coming to get us."

"Don't like snakes much," I said. I squinted up at the ledges. I expected a horde of rattlers to come sliding out of the rocks and drop down into the river. "Hope no rattlers come swimming up to our raft."

"Nope," Jasper said, grinning. "Won't see any this trip. Water's too high, too cold."

I looked at the ledges on Jasper's side. "Don't know about that, Jasper," I said, sounding real excited. "Look yonder. There's one dropping into the water now."

"Wh-where?" Jasper's mouth dropped open, and he turned his head real quick.

This time *I* laughed.

"Guess I deserved that," Jasper said sheepishly. Then he laughed, too. Wasn't anything so good as having Jasper for a friend.

The sun was slipping down behind the Pennsylvania hills, turning the mountains a deep purple. By turns, we tugged on our coats and grabbed some crullers from the hamper to tide us over.

Rastus walked up to see how we were faring. Asked if we could manage to push on after dark. Asked if he could spell me. My pa could manage alone at the rear, he said. Didn't want to give up my oar, though. Didn't want to show any weakness. I was tuckered out but feeling too good to give up. "I'm fine, Rastus," I said. "Plenty fine. Thanks all the same."

"You got pluck, son," Rastus said. "Glad to have you along." He squeezed my shoulder, walked across to visit with Jasper while he munched on a cruller.

We passed through Long Eddy, where a lot of rafts had tied up for the night, but I was glad we didn't stop. Far as I could tell, we were the only ones still out on the river.

The moon came up, cast mysterious light over the

mountains, and reflected palely against the water. The river moved so fast that it seemed to take the moonlight along with it.

It was chilly now. Our breath made small clouds in the night air. A lonesome quietness settled around us, cast a sort of spell with the long black shadows and the lulling sound of water and the dipping of oars.

I had to shake myself awake. I could barely stand, my legs were numb, my knees wanted to buckle. Pa still pushed on.

Someone started to sing. In the shadowy moonlight, it took me a minute to realize my pa was the one singing. I hadn't heard him sing since before Ma first took sick more than six months ago. Seemed longer though. The tune was mournful, or maybe it was the moonlight that made it so sad and beautiful. He was singing "Red River Valley." Never thought of it as being a sorrowful song, but it was tonight; it was in Pa's voice:

> *"From this valley they say you are going,*
> *We will miss your bright eyes and sweet smile,*
> *For they say you are taking the sunshine,*
> *That has brightened our pathway awhile."*

I'd never heard him sing "Red River Valley," though it was a song I had learned at school and sung at home sometimes. Pa used to sing "My Old Kentucky Home" to us when he got back from his rafting trips, only Pa said Pepacton, not Kentucky.

Once I'd heard him sing a song about a blackbird and a maid with golden hair. Couldn't say if it was the shaft of moonlight spilling through the window that woke me or Pa's voice filling the quiet. At first, when I peered out, he and Ma were sitting under the plum tree. Then Pa stood up and pulled Ma to her feet and into his arms. Around they waltzed, passing by the cabin close enough for me to see their happiness.

Now all Pa had for a dancing partner was a wooden oar. I listened to his lonesome voice going out through the darkness; sometimes it came echoing back from a far-away place.

Jasper was still. We all were, just listening. Then Pa stopped. He called for us to pull Jersey for Dreamers' Island, then pull back hard the other way to miss the Jersey rocks. We went on by Callicoon and tied up at Bush's Eddy just below. The only tavern there was a temperance one, and that didn't suit Pa or Rastus. So we hiked back to Callicoon on a worn path, up a steep embankment, over the railroad tracks to a hotel where thirsty raftsmen were welcomed. My first day on the river was done.

Before we had our meal, I crumpled from the weariness. Strong arms lifted me. Couldn't even say whose. I dropped my head against the rough wool of an overcoat and fell into a dreamless sleep.

Chapter Fifteen

Sometimes you know a day is going to be bad when you wake up. Sort of like a wool blanket scratching against your bare skin that you can't shake off, nohow, even after you get up.

I felt that way this morning. Maybe it was waking up and being the only girl in a room full of snoring men. Can't say for sure, but I did have that uneasiness scratching at me. I was awake before the rest, having slept more than my fair share already. I slipped out of the room and found my way to the facilities out back.

The moon was going down; clouds were rolling in out of the north, turning the air damp and raw, gusty, too.

Coming back, I smelled breakfast — ham, bacon, biscuits, who knows what all — warming up the gray dawn.

The side door of the hotel was cracked open; I peeked my head inside, knowing it was the kitchen.

"Why lookee here, girls. It's the sweet-faced lad who fell asleep at the table last night. Missed his supper, too." A girl about the same age as Jasper's oldest sister pulled me inside. When she whirled back around, her long single braid swished against her back. Tied on the end of the braid was a purple satin ribbon. Ma's purple. I sucked in my breath and reached out a hand, touched it with the tips of my fingers. When I saw the cook eyeing me, I drew back like I'd been slapped. I put my head down and kept my mouth shut, didn't try to explain a thing, just the way Jasper had told me to do if I thought trouble was brewing.

Inside was another girl, a little older yet. I glanced cautiously at the cook. She was a short woman with thick eyebrows and dark hair on her upper lip. She stood on a low stool and flipped griddlecakes over a large black stove.

"Begging your pardon," I said, removing my hat, "if you please, I sure could use a wash-up." I looked from face to face. Easy enough to see by their coloring and profusion of hair that they were family, a mother with two daughters of courting age.

"My, my, we got us a proper gent, fine looking, too. Too bad he ain't older." They had a time giggling over that. Girls sure could act foolish over a boy.

The younger girl, the one who had drawn me into the room, led me over to the sink. I took off my coat, rolled up my sleeves, and grabbed the bar of Fels Napatha. Didn't know what to do then.

They laughed. "Imagine that, a Hill Hawk with manners. Bet you never saw a water pump before," the older daughter said.

"No'm," I said.

"Don't mind us." The younger one worked the handle of the pump till water spilled into the sink. It was something, seeing water come right inside that way. I scrubbed my arms, my hands, my face. Took off my hat and washed my head. The water was as icy as the water I carried in buckets from our spring near the cabin. I didn't mind. It was warm in the kitchen, and the women liked making a pet of me. Figured if they'd known I was a girl, they wouldn't have fussed so much.

They sat me down at a worktable near the stove, brought me a tin cup of hot coffee and a plate piled with griddlecakes, eggs and home fries, biscuits with sausage gravy, a thick slice of ham, and applesauce. I set to eating like I hadn't had a decent meal in months. In a way, that was true enough.

They bustled around me, piling food on large platters, covering them up, putting them on the warming shelf over the stove. This was a fine place, fine people. When her girls went out to set up the dining room for breakfast, the cook stepped down from her stool and came over, studied me hard. "Saw you coveting that purple ribbon," she said. "You got the prettiest blue eyes I ever did see, slender hands, an uncommon virtue for cleanliness. You got a secret, doncha, blue-eyed boy?" she said softly, her eyes snapping. "Wonder what I'd find if I snatched your overalls down."

I wet my lips, shifted my eyes toward the door. I could hear the men coming into the dining room, and the good-natured laughter of her girls. In another minute they'd be coming through those swinging doors. In another minute they would know, and, then, so would everyone else — Jasper, his pa, and every river man.

The cook studied my face. "It'd be hell to pay for your pa if the men found out. They'd likely gang up on him for bringing along a girl. Rafting is man's play."

Didn't know what to say, hung my head, fearful that something bad might happen to Pa.

She pressed a finger lightly into the middle of my chest. "Awful risky you messing in men's business," she said softly. "Guess your pa must have his reasons." She shook her head and scowled as if she were trying to cipher it out. "Don't worry, little girl, I won't tell no one you're not a boy."

I just nodded. I didn't rightly know why Pa had brought me along. Figured he needed my help. Thankfully, her girls came barreling back through the door with their warm laughter, and I didn't have to answer.

"Scoot now, but take care," the cook whispered. Her words spooked me all right. The greasy breakfast churned in my stomach. Outside, red the color of blood smeared the morning horizon. Didn't need Pa or anyone to tell me it was an omen of storm.

Sobered, I went out and sat at the end of the long dining table while the rest of the men ate. They were somber this morning, kept their heads down, didn't talk. Rafts men had a sense about the weather. Everybody knew it was not going to be an easy day on the river.

I took Ma's diary and wrote her about the trip so far. Told her about Fannie Read and about the wondrous river. Told her how we rafted in the moonlight and how Pa had sung again for the first. Told her Pa missed her; I missed her, too. Told her I was doing okay. Told her I was losing some of my meanness. Then I wrote about the cook.

The cook here at the Delaware House and her two daughters made a big fuss over me, Ma. Called me sweet-faced, said I had the prettiest blue eyes. Made me feel like maybe I was getting my girl looks like you always said I would. Not sure they know what proper girl looks are, though. They had their girl shapes all right, but they were in dire need of a shave.

I knew Ma would like the part about my girl looks. I didn't tell her the rest, about the bad feeling I'd had since getting up or about the cook knowing I was a girl and how that could be trouble for Pa. Maybe it'd be trouble for me, too.

A light drizzle had started to fall when we left the hotel and made our way along the slippery banks of the river. We turned up our collars, hunched in our coats, turned the brims down on our hats. We took our places on the raft, pushed off from the shore without saying more than a word.

Chapter Sixteen

The wind came howling down the river, hurried our raft
even faster. Jasper and I got the worst of it, the gusts
driving rain into our faces. No way to help it. Fog mixed
with the drizzle, making it even harder to see. The water
was choppy, tossing the raft, making it hard to hold on
course. I was starting to shake from the cold.

Pa was in a black mood. Couldn't blame him. When
he hollered, his voice was like a whip. "Pull Jersey, pull
hard." There was no music in any of us today except for
our jangling nerves.

Jasper hollered over to me, "Don't fall!" That's what I
thought he said, but then I heard the roar and knew we
were headed into a falls. The river narrowed, and the
water surged through the channel, thundering down the

rapids over boulders jutting up on the Pennsylvania side. The current was powerful. How could Pa steer? We'd ram the rocks for sure.

Pa's voice was lost in the violent rage of wind and water, but he signaled, making sharp jabs to pull left to the Jersey side. Rain pelted our faces, blinded us nearly. I couldn't see his hand signs for sure, but I was scared and pulled away from the boulders as hard as I could.

I wanted to run to the center of the raft, run from the water frothing around us, hissing and sloshing and spilling onto the deck as if it would drag us under. The raft would surely be torn apart, broken to splinters, and all of us with it. We were going to die. I was going to die. I clung to my oar as if it could save me.

I opened my mouth to scream, but my voice was gone. I didn't know which way to turn, which way to pull. I just hung on.

"Hold the oars," Pa hollered.

I did with all my might. I flung myself down over the oar, hit the deck, and clung to one of the lash poles that fastened the logs together. Just in time, too. The front of the raft went over the edge of the falls and the bow tipped down. The force of the wild current tugged, pulled the bow and me with it straight toward the bottom. Water boomed in my ears. Or was it the logs breaking apart? The bow drove downward even more, and I thought the water was going to swallow me up.

All at once, the front of the raft popped right out of the depths, and on we rode through those furious rapids. All I did was hang on and pray that Pa knew what he was doing. He did. The ride was quick, but long enough for me to learn that my pa could fly steady and sure like a hawk.

The river widened out.

"Jeepers," Jasper shouted, when we had moved away from the tumbling water. "Harley, you okay?" he called.

My legs wobbled, felt as sloshy as the water. Didn't know how I could stand at all. Guess I had my river legs all right. "Nope," I yelled back. "How 'bout you?"

"Heck no," Jasper called.

We laughed, our voices ringing out over the raging of water and wind. Nothing like the good feeling of safety after a danger was passed. Lord, it did make me joyful.

Pa and Rastus passed the jug. Thought it might help me and Jasper, too, but none was offered to the hands at the front.

It grew colder. The rain turned to snow, a heavy, wet snow. We passed through a smoother stretch for a ways, long enough for my legs to feel strong again. The snow stuck to our coats and overalls, froze them stiff. My fingers burned with cold inside my soggy gloves. Didn't know how we could keep going, but Pa pushed on.

We pulled Jersey and passed Horse Island on the left. We pulled to the right, crossed over to the west, passed Hog Island on that side, pulled Jersey again to pass through Prayer Rock Rift.

Pa hollered, "Pull. Pull hard. All hands pull." Ahead, the river narrowed with high rock ledges on either side. The channel was blocked, jammed high with ice and littered with timber from broken rafts. Barrels and kegs, lumber and other rafting debris floundered in the choppy water.

Pa steered for the New York side at Narrowsburg. We put to shore, securing our raft upstream from the ice jam and from the eddy overflowing with rafts already tied up. Wondered how many days they'd been waiting on the ice.

"Nine mile we come. Nine mile." Pa shook his head in disgust, spouted some mighty strong oaths. We were stuck all right. All we could do was wait for the ice jam to break up. Shoulders slumped, we tramped up the steep path to the town.

All I could think about was a place to get warm and dry, but the taverns were overflowing. We tramped through the mud and slush until we found one with room to spare on the outskirts of town. The men took a gander at our frozen condition and the way opened for us straight to the stove.

We shed our coats and stood by the stove to thaw out. I was thinking about the bad feeling I'd had at the start of the day, when a big red-haired man shouted at us from the bar. "That you, Amos Basket?"

Pa scowled but didn't say a word.

"Amos, you hear me?"

Pa didn't show any sign he was being hailed.

"Amos, that scrawny pup standing there by you looks awful sweet, sweet enough to be a girl. That your son or what?"

I felt Pa stiffen, saw his hands curl into fists.

I curled my hands into fists, too. Wasn't going to let that river man think I was a girl. I'd show him. I took a step forward, but Jasper grabbed my arm and yanked me back. "Let it go," he said quietly.

Knew Jasper was right. Only thing I couldn't keep still was my heart. I chewed my lip and worried that Pa was in for big trouble, that they'd all gang up on him like the cook had warned.

Silence spread over the tavern. Nobody talked. No one moved, not even to raise a mug of beer. They were all watching, their eyes darting from Pa to the man at the bar; they were waiting for Pa to make a move.

"That pup has lots more spine than you, Gabe," Pa said.

The man sneered. "That so?"

"Ayah," Pa said calmly.

"Fools like you ought to buy a round of drinks for the wise men who know enough to stay out of a storm," the man said to rile Pa.

I started calculating the chance we'd have in a brawl — four of us against thirty, maybe forty of them. Pa was bigger than most of the men, bigger than the loudmouth.

"Ain't scared of you," Pa said.

The man moved away from the bar, swaggered toward us. "Don't take kindly to being called spineless, Amos. Guess I'm gonna have to rearrange you some for that."

I edged closer to Jasper, grabbed his arm. Pa took a step forward, his arms loose at his sides. "Don't want to fight you, Gabe."

The man danced in front of us, his fists up and ready.

He threw light jabs at Pa. Pa ducked them. The man laughed. "I heard you could fight," Gabe said.

"Guess you heard wrong," Pa said.

Gabe threw a hard right. Pa caught the man's wrist, twisted him around real fast, kicked him in the backside. Gabe went sprawling on his face.

"Told you, Gabe, I don't want to fight," Pa said, as the man, red-faced, got to his feet. "We'll take those drinks you offered and thankee."

The place exploded with laughter. All the men were shouting, "The drinks are on Gabe."

I saw the anger flicker in Gabe's eyes. Hoped we wouldn't cross his path on this trip again.

The door blew open and Lew Hawley with the peg leg came in with his brothers from Downsville. "Storm's over, men," he shouted.

Everyone piled out the door. Clouds drifted apart; sunlight and blue sky spilled through. Clear weather and sunshine, and we were still stuck in Narrowsburg waiting on the river to push the ice jam on through the narrows.

My bad feeling left, though. That night I went to sleep feeling good about my spine and my pa.

Chapter Seventeen

The ice went out in the middle of the night. The thundering of it woke up the men except for the ones passed out from too much red-eye.

We were bedded down on a floor covered with hay, and packed together like pickles in a jar. Pa and Rastus put Jasper and me between them, so we weren't sleeping next to any drunken strangers. After the commotion, I couldn't sleep. I waited a bit till the talking stopped and the snoring took over again. Then I nudged Jasper with an elbow. "You awake?" I whispered.

"Yup," he said.

"Got to ask you a question."

"All right."

I edged closer so I could whisper directly in his ear. Didn't want Pa to hear me, nohow. "My pa," I said. "Is he always like this on a river trip?"

"Like what?"

"Well, he doesn't seem to be much of a fighter, not like you said. And does he sing, usually?"

Jasper was quiet, thinking it over, maybe. "He's different this trip, more particular of his manners."

"That good or bad?"

"Different, like I said, Harley."

I tried to sleep, but there was more I needed to know. I could tell by Jasper's squirming and jagged breathing that he was still awake, too.

"Jasper?" I moved close to him again. "Can I ask you something?"

"All right."

"I was wondering . . . what would Pa have done to Gabe, say, if I hadn't been along?"

"Don't know for sure. Some fool challenges him once every trip, I'd say. Sometimes your pa fights, and sometimes he don't. This time, he was just protecting and defending you. If he'd wanted to cause a fracas, he'd have stepped up to fight. That's sort of a signal for river men to join in."

119

"So what's the difference between a boot to the backside or a fist to the chin?"

"Harley, ain't you ever seen a real brawl b'fore?"

"Nope, just little fistfights at school," I said.

Jasper gave a low whistle. He sighed. "If your pa had punched Gabe, then everybody would have jumped in to fight, too. See, your pa made Gabe look like the fool he was. So . . . no fight."

"Will Gabe try to fight Pa again?" I asked, remembering how he had looked so wrathful at Pa.

"Naw," Jasper said. "Probably won't pick on anybody or even show his face for a good time to come."

"Pa did all that?"

"Yup," Jasper said. "We'd better catch some sleep, now," he said, yawning. "Tomorrow's going to be a lo-o-ng one."

I turned on my side away from Jasper and closed my eyes, thought about everything Jasper had told me. This time Jasper nudged me. "Hey, Harley, you awake?"

"Yup."

"Forgot to tell you about the dam at Lackawaxen we'll be going over tomorrow. It's darn scary. When your pa says hold, you hold tight, Harley. Don't let go or you'll lose your footing, get thrown overboard sure enough."

"When Pa says hold, hold tight," I echoed.

"You got to trust your pa. He'll get us over safe, but you got to do your part. Just hold on tight."

"Hold tight," I whispered. This time I dropped right off, dreamed about riding on the water, dreamed I was the one steering the raft, dreamed Pa was singing that song to me from somewhere far away, and that someone was crying for help.

When I woke up, Pa was leaning over me, talking in a low voice, saying it was time to get up, cautioned me to be quiet. The four of us slipped from the room, went downstairs to get some breakfast. The food was ready except for the eggs. We ate in a hurry, then headed out.

The sky was putting on its pale morning dress as we clambered aboard the raft. There was no wind. We were the first ones to the river. We didn't have to wait or fight or position with the dozens of other rafts that would be moving out within the next hour. It was going to be a warm spring day. We were all in fine spirits as we shoved off.

There were islands and bridge piers to navigate around — the Erie Railroad crossed over the river to the Pennsylvania side — then rapids and another rift, then we came up on a wide eddy at Ten-Mile River.

"Hey, boy, come here," Pa hollered, motioning to me with his hand.

I wet my lips, gave Jasper a questioning look. He shrugged. Didn't know of anything I'd done wrong.

"Come on." Pa was impatient this time.

Feeling a bit queasy, I walked toward the rear of the raft. The ride was smooth though, the water burbled and hurried along, but there was no wind to ruff it up, no rapids in sight. May have been the sweetest water we'd rafted.

When I reached Pa, he looked serious but not mad. "Get on up here next to me," he growled.

Guess I was going get chewed on for something. I bit down on my lip. My legs got wobbly; my stomach churned like white-water waves were crashing in it. "What you want?" I asked.

"Thought maybe you'd like to try steering for a spell." His voice was gentler now.

I nodded and got up next to him, stood with my hand on the oar. Pa stayed right behind me, covering his hand over mine. We rode like that for a ways. Didn't think I'd ever been that close to Pa since Ma died, except when he had a mind to cuff me. That was strange. "You got the feel of it?" he asked.

"Ayah," I said. "'Bout like steering a sled that's flying downhill over the snow."

"Yup, that's it," Pa said. He chuckled like he'd been tickled good. Then Pa took his hands away, stepped back, and I was steersman. It was glorious. Better than a birthday, better than winning a spelling bee. I knew it was an easy stretch, the way we glided along slick as anything, but I still felt the power of the river coming up through that oar, the danger and the thrill. Pa took the other rear oar, and Rastus walked up to the front with Jasper.

"Pull Pennsylvania," I hollered, and they did. Could be that I was the only girl steering a raft on this whole mighty river. That was really something. "Holt t'other way," I yelled, and they did that, too.

Soon enough, Pa came back over. "You got the gift," he whispered.

I glanced up quick, met his eyes. Didn't have a proud look, though, just a real sad one. I waited, but he didn't say anything more.

"Thankee," I said. I put my head down and walked to the front. Guessed maybe Pa was never going to call me his girl again.

Right after, we ran through a bunch of trouble spots — a place with high hills on either shore with bad rocks on the Jersey side, a few small islands, and a mighty big tributary that had rafts moving into the main river — but all those places seemed more like riding a sled downhill, trying to steer around a stump or like readying yourself for the thrill of flying over sudden bumps or rises in the hill. I was getting to be a seasoned rafter all right. That's when Pa yelled, "Holt!" And I did.

The bow of the raft shot out over the edge of a low dam in a flat section of the river, but the water seemed to be running high enough to carry us over the top. Was the raft moving slower? Was it hung up on the dam? There we were, stuck in midair on the top of the dam. Then the front teetered, tipped down; below us I could see the angry, tumbling water waiting to grab us. "Yikes," I yelled. I clung to the oar and tried to keep from sliding.

"Hold the oars and hit the deck," Pa hollered.

I quick raised my oar, slammed my body face-down on top of it, grabbed a lash pole, and wrapped my fingers around it.

The front of the raft crashed down, made a fierce splash into the roiling waters. Water poured over me, covering me with its angry arms. But I wasn't so scared now. I knew those watery arms would have to let me go. All I had to do was hold tight.

All at once, the bow of the raft popped up like before and the water ran off. We were soaked but safe. Jasper, too. We leapt to our feet and carried on with a loud hurrah.

No sooner had I got my wind again than Pa hollered, "Pull Jersey!" to miss the piers of the Roebling Aqueduct of the D&H Canal.

I did like Pa ordered. Knew he could be trusted to breathe with the river, knew I could do my part, too. We rode the river like hawks riding the wind, free and easy, soaring with the gladness of being alive.

We made good time all that day, passing some wondrous crags and bluffs, stands of deep uncut forests, sprawling farms with meadows and pastures of grazing sheep and cows, villages of pretty houses and picket fences, churches and steeples, wide eddies, and islands. Pa let me take the oar to steer more than once, let me maneuver around an island even. We stopped at Milford for our midday meal, then shoved on to Dingman's Ferry, where we tied up for the night. Like Jasper said, rafting was a darn good frolic.

Chapter Eighteen

Jasper kept to himself during supper that night. Didn't talk, sat eating with his head down. Missed his friendly grin and ways. Didn't know till now how much I counted on Jasper for his generous nature. Figured I knew what was ailing him. Guessed he was jealous 'cause I'd gotten to steer and he hadn't.

"Hey, Jasper," I said, when the men had finished eating and had settled down to drinking and talking. "Want to go for a walk, look around some?"

"All right," he said, not smiling.

We stepped out of the tavern and walked down to the shore. It was a fair spring evening, past twilight now. We'd traveled far enough south that the wild cherry trees were in blossom, and the air was sweet and clean. Lamp-light from the village homes was beginning to make patterns of light in the dusk. It was a pleasing sight.

"What's ailing you, Jasper?" I asked.

"Nothing I care to talk about," he said.

"You mad at me?"

"Naw."

"You can steer tomorrow."

"That's not it, Harley. I've done it plenty of times."

"Oh."

The river eddy was wide and peaceful here. We watched the water rippling past, tossed stones, tried to see how far we could throw.

"Jasper?" I said, perching on a large rock.

"Yeah?" he said, coming to sit down next to me.

"You and I, we could raft together."

Jasper shook his head, leaned to the side, and scooped up some small stones. "Nope," he said.

"No?"

"Pa's quitting. You heard him. Told me himself, that this is his last season to raft. Doesn't want to go anymore. Says he's got more important things to consider. Lost his nerve, I guess." Jasper pitched rocks like he aimed to hurt something now.

"You could go rafting with me and my pa. Can't do much else this time of year."

"Guess I could . . ." Jasper shrugged, took one of his stones, and pitched it hard, far out into the eddy.

Jasper shifted around to face me. "We're friends, right?"

"Right."

"Good friends," he said slowly.

"Best," I said.

"Right," he said. He was quiet.

"Right," I echoed. Behind us, I could hear the noise from the tavern. The sound of the river breathing in front of us, my own and Jasper's, too.

"So . . . best friends need to trust each other, right?"

"Right," I said slowly.

"So . . . you got something you want to tell me?" he asked, pitching another stone into the current.

I wet my lips, my heart pounding like we were going over the Lackawaxen dam again. "Maybe . . ." I took a raggedy breath. "You have something particular in mind?"

"Might," Jasper said. My skin tingled like I was breaking out with hives. I had a pretty fair idea what he might be thinking. If I was right, he might not want to be my friend. He might even despise me. I swallowed hard.

Jasper reached over and took my hand. "That man back in Narrowsburg was right. You are awful sweet looking. You got slender hands . . ."

"And no Adam's apple." I hung my head.

"How come?" Jasper said, sort of roughlike.

I gulped. "'Cause I'm no boy. I'm a mean, short-haired girl."

Jasper looked away from me and out across the water. I heard him sigh. He must be real sorry about that. "That might be what I was wondering," Jasper said finally.

"When did you guess?"

"Never guessed. Knew from the start. Your pa told us. Figured since you chopped off your hair, you could go along with us as a boy. Said it'd be better if we all kept it a secret. Safer for you. Less risky for us. That's part of it anyway."

I yanked my hand away and pushed him off the rock. I stood up and looked down at him. "You mean to tell me that you knew and you were just teasing me about shooting rifles and hair on my chest and all that other stuff just to make me stew and fret that you'd figure it out?"

Jasper grinned. "Sure," he said.

"Oh?" I leapt down next to him and pushed him

again. "But since you knew all along, you should have told me. When I see Pa, I'm going to . . ."

"No!" Jasper said in alarm. He sighed. "I promised your pa. Don't want him thinking he can't trust his crew."

I scowled and backed away. I shook my head and kicked at the loose stones on the shore.

"It'll be our secret. I won't tell if you don't," Jasper said.

"All right," I said grudgingly.

"Good," Jasper said. "Now, what I want to know is why *you* didn't tell me? Did you promise your pa?"

"No, not exactly," I said slowly.

"Wasn't nothing keeping you from telling me," Jasper said, sounding injured. "So . . . why didn't you?"

"'Cause I was afraid you wouldn't be my friend if you found out I was a girl."

"Guess you were wrong."

"Glad I was wrong," I said, feeling like a real big log had rolled off me. "I'd like it fine if you taught me to shoot, took me fishing."

"I'd like that, too. I like you an awful lot, Hattie Belle," he said with a catch in his voice.

My heart soared when he said my true name out loud.

I was Hattie Belle again and Jasper was still my best friend. That was really something.

"Guess we'd better get on back to the tavern," he said.

"Guess we'd better," I echoed. We started back, walking close, our shoulders rubbing together. I was feeling real good, thinking about how fine things were turning out for me and Jasper.

"We only got us one more day this trip," Jasper said. He didn't sound glad about that.

When we were almost to the tavern, Jasper asked, "You still hate him, your pa?" he asked.

"No," I said. "Guess I don't. Maybe all that meanness washed out of me back there at the Lackawaxen dam."

"That's a good thing, real good," Jasper said. "'Cause he don't hate you, Hattie Belle. All he wanted was to keep you safe. By now, you gotta know yourself that saloons with wild river men are no place for girls."

I didn't say anything. Didn't want to, 'cause I was wrong and Jasper was right. Didn't know for sure how Pa felt, though. Didn't think he hated me anymore, but he still didn't call me his girl, either.

Chapter Nineteen

When we left the inn the next morning, the sky was thick with charcoal-bellied clouds. "Gonna be no sun t'day," Pa noted as we shoved off. A sort of gray gloom hovered around us even though it was warm.

We hadn't gone far downriver before the wind started sweeping upriver, skimmed across the surface, pushed against the raft, pushed hard like it didn't want us to go any farther. Slowed us down all right.

We rode through some real pretty country, though. Pa asked me if I wanted to steer for a bit. I was willing. Pa nodded, smiled for once like I'd baked him an honest-to-goodness plum pie.

He stood behind me again like the day before. Told me to get the feel of the raft and the oar, to calculate the wind and the water. The wind was troubling, made the raft harder to hold on to whatever course was set.

I steered us on by where the Bushkill came in from the Pennsylvania side. At the mouth of the river, a lot of men were trying to fish, but the wind was whipping their lines. They were real intent, didn't even seem to see us going by. Wondered that they were even out here on a day like this.

We passed a column of rock rising out of the river that looked like a stack of books. I kept on going till we passed the little village of Flat Brook. Then Pa took over again. I was ready, too. The wind blew straight in my face, stung my eyes, made them weep.

We pushed on under the dark, forboding sky. Then, suddenly, the wind stopped, and I became still with silent awe as we came up on the Shawangunk Mountain, towering above us like a mighty rock of ages. How small I was, we were, on our river raft, as we paddled through this giant walled gap in the river.

The water was dark here and deep; the current less troubled. For once, I liked seeing where we'd been, instead of being so anxious about what lay ahead. As I dipped my oar and pulled to Pa's commands, my eyes stayed bound to the rocky glory of the gap, the grand hotels perched on the high bluffs above.

After we moved out of the gap, the wind died and we made better time. Pa pulled up to the Jersey side at a town called Belvidere for our dinner. It was already well past noon. While we were eating the last of the food we'd brought from home, Pa warned me about the stretch ahead, said it was the most feared and dangerous rift in the river. "Little Foul Rift is first," Pa said. "Then a short stretch of slack water before Big Foul Rift. We'll be pulling Pennsylvania all the way. There's shallow water and rock reefs on the Jersey side, and jagged limestone jutting about three feet high on the opposite shore. But the water on the Pennsylvania side is deep. We'll go into the rift about forty feet from that shore.

"It's gonna look like we're headed into those rocks on the right shore, and you'll want to pull to the Jersey side, but you gotta keep your head. The water is going to be thundering in your ears, so watch for my hand signals." Pa stopped, smoothed his mustache as if considering. "Don't be counting on it even for a second, but if I can line up the raft, and we enter the channel in the favorable spot I know, I'll give you a thumbs-up. Might be able to pilot through that second rift without you having to pull on the oars. Done it before. Just can't know for sure what's ahead."

"Like the raft in the channel at Enoch Island or the fleet coming down from the west branch," I said.

"Ayah," Pa said. "The rifts with slack water between are about three mile all told, and it'll take about a quarter-hour to get through it. It's the most perilous place, the worst in our journey. Hold tight to your oar, stand firm, and keep your eye on me."

"I will, Pa," I said. "Like a hawk."

Pa grinned at that, but looked sober all the same. Jasper didn't say a word, and his pa just chewed on his sandwich, his face white and grim with dread.

This time before we pushed off, we made sure every-thing was tied down snug.

"Don't get rattled, no matter what," Jasper warned. "Don't look around, just keep your eyes fixed on your pa. We'll get through it, and be pleased with our courage 'fore you know it," Jasper said. He mustered a grin, but he looked spooked all the same.

My heart was already pounding as we left the safe cove at Belvidere, pounding so hard I wouldn't have been able to hear if Pa was hollering. My breath was short and choppy like waves from a gust of wind. Except for Pa, we were all about to bust from fright.

"Pull Pennsylvania, pull hard," Pa called when we were about a half mile from the first channel. Out of the corner of my eye, I saw a raft in front veering to the left, drifting over to the Jersey side of the channel. With a sinking heart, I knew if that raft got hung up on the reefs, it would swing out into the channel and block our path.

Above the roaring of the rapids, I heard another sound, the cracking and splitting sound of timber crashing into rocks. It was in front of us where I couldn't see. But Pa could.

He signaled to keep pulling Pennsylvania, pull hard. I did, though we were closing in on the jagged limestone of that shore. If I pulled much more, the watery fists of the rapids would grab us and pummel us against the rocks. Pa was hollering. I couldn't hear what he was saying, but I knew it was trouble. I butted the toes of my boots tight up against a lash pole and steadied myself with the oar.

Thump! I felt the Jersey side of our raft, Jasper's side, slam into something hard. I was jolted forward, but my footing held and I didn't tumble over or lose hold of my oar. I wanted to holler out to Jasper, look to see if he was okay, but Pa was giving furious signals to keep pulling Pennsylvania. Pa was like a hawk — talons extended, wings set, eyes piercing its prey — intent on finding safe passage through the white water.

By now, the angry water was tugging our raft toward the jagged limestone, but Pa kept signaling for us to pull. Keep your head, I told myself. I pulled hard, watched as we closed in on the rocky shore. Trust Pa.

In the space of a breath, Pa signaled again. This time to Jersey. I pivoted my oar, pulled real hard the other way. I was cheered by the sight of Jasper standing steady and strong. No logs on our raft had broken away. Pa had safely piloted us through.

As our raft plunged on through the rift, I saw the other raft, crashed up against hidden rocks, its backside swinging crosswise in the angry rapids of the channel. A few of the logs had broken from their lashing, and a man and a boy were working with poles to set their raft free. There was no way for us to help; the current pulled us swiftly onward.

We got through Little Foul Rift and safely into the slack water. I was hoping Pa would put to shore here, but he was looking ahead, calculating, I guess, his favored entry point for Big Foul Rift. Can't say how glad I was when he gave Jasper and me the thumbs-up signal. I gave him a thumbs-up back, took a quick glance at Jasper. He was grinning, but bracing his feet and holding his oar like me for the ride to come.

This time, when we entered the churning rift, the hair rose up on the back of my neck. The drops were deeper; white water roared all around us. The raft surged and plunged, bounced and plowed on. All the time I kept my eyes on Pa, waiting for him to signal if he needed me to pull the oar.

The damaged raft came barreling into the rapids behind us. I got a real bad feeling when I saw it. From what Pa had told me, I knew the raft was too far on the Jersey side, not even close to the furrow Pa had plowed. Why didn't they follow our path?

The bow of our raft shot up in the white water, crashed down; water poured over the deck, covering me up to my knees, sprayed over my head, soaked me. I clenched my teeth together to keep from shrieking. The water screamed around us like a pack of hungry beasts. But I heard the other scream, thought it was me or Jasper crying out in fear. But it wasn't.

Then I saw. Saw that damaged raft crack, splinter to

pieces like kindling sticks on the hidden reefs. Saw those big timbers spreading apart in the front where the boy was standing, a boy built sturdy, strong like Jasper with dark hair like his, too. He wore a red kerchief around his neck, and his face was white as the pages in Ma's journal. I sucked in my breath and held it when the pilot, face gone gray as ash, threw a rope. It swung out across the water, arced through the air, closed the space between the man and the boy. I willed it to reach that boy. He grabbed for it, but the rope fell short, dropped into the water. I gasped and gripped my oar even tighter.

The boy struggled to keep his footing on the crippled deck, but he slipped. His feet flew out as the logs pulled away and tumbled over and over in the rolling rapids. I saw the terror on his face when he was gripped by the foaming jaws of water and pulled under, saw him come up, his arms flailing in the angry rapids, saw his mouth open to scream, saw it fill with water, saw the frothing jaws close over his head and swallow him. He did not come up again. My eyes misted over, but I still heard the wrenching cry of the man and the crash as the crippled raft broke to pieces on the reefs.

Pa piloted us to shore in the eddy just below the rift. Men were waiting there with jugs of whiskey, but the news we gave sent them scurrying upriver. I looked at the others; nobody had to say, "Did you see . . ." It was plain we all knew. I walked a ways from the others, retched under some straggly bushes, started to shake, felt so cold I couldn't stop trembling.

Pa came over, squatted down by me, drew me to my feet, sat me down on a rock, wiped my face, wrapped his coat around me, chafed my hands with his trembling fingers. "Weren't nothing I could do to save that boy. Only thing I could do was save my own crew. Got to believe that littleun," he said, his face pale and sorrowful.

"I know it, Pa." I nodded, tears clouding my eyes.

"All right then," he said. "Hard as it is, we got to get back out there on the river. Keeping on is the only way to get through."

There were no whiskey jugs this time, just grieving. Pa loosened the rope and we paddled back into the river, pushing on to Easton to end our day.

PART IV

⊰ Journey's End ⊱

Chapter Twenty

That night in Easton, Jasper and I stayed awake and talked about the tragedy of that boy drowning in Big Foul Rift long after the last of the rafts men had bedded down for the night. Sleep seemed fearful. Didn't want to close my eyes. Couldn't put that poor boy's face out of my head, the sight and sound of the raft breaking to pieces around him, the cries of both, man and boy. I was glad the boy wasn't Jasper. Glad it wasn't any one of us. Pa had saved our hides.

Earlier, Pa had told us that man had no business on the river. Any river man could have told him about Foul Rift, Pa said. "He could've followed me." Pa cussed a good deal, clenched his fists. "If I didn't know every rift and rock and island in the river," Pa said, "I'd never risk it with a child, 'specially my own."

I felt real good when Pa said that. It was pretty near like having him call me his girl.

Jasper and I were quiet for a time, but I could tell by his breathing that he was still awake. Guess we were both just grieving for that boy. The snoring of Pa and Rastus was comforting and of all the men around who had come safely through. I didn't have the heart to write anything about the lost boy in Ma's diary. All I wrote was *Pa got us safely through the Foul Rifts. You'd been so proud of him, Ma.*

"Jasper?" I asked, a catch in my voice. "Did you know that my ma died?"

"Yup," Jasper said.

"Did Pa tell you?"

"Said she died. That's about all. He said your ma wouldn't want everybody coming and making a fuss. She'd just want to rest peaceful-like. He figured it was best left that way for you and him, too. Your pa never invited much talk unless it had to do with logging or rafting. He was different after your ma died, though, quieter."

"Yeah," I said. "Didn't sing or smile anymore. Didn't do much but grunt and cuss."

"What was she like, your ma?"

"Sweet — a good sweet. You know, like when you bite into a plum and the juice tickles your tongue and you lick your lips so you don't lose a single drop, and you kind of shiver 'cause it's the best thing you've tasted in a year? Ma was sweet like that all the time, to me and Pa," I said in a hushed voice. "She was gentle with proper manners and a way of speaking words that made it seem as if they were created just for her to say. 'Please,' she would say, and 'Thank you,' and 'You must sit like this and walk like that, hold a cup this way and a fork that way.' Tried to teach me. Never stuck to me. Guess I'm too much like Pa."

Jasper raised up on one elbow. "You have a way of putting words together real good, too. Better than a schoolteacher. Guess you're like your ma that way. Glad you don't have fussy manners, though. That could get real hard on a fella after a while."

Glad it was dark so Jasper couldn't see how I blushed over that. No one had ever told me I had any likeness to Ma before.

"How'd she die, your ma?" Jasper asked.

I choked on that. Couldn't say for a minute. "She had a cough and sharp pains in her side; pleurisy, Pa said. It

145

didn't want to let go of her. She was sad, too. I couldn't cheer her up, nohow. One day she just stopped taking the cure. Laid herself down and quit on me. Guess, maybe, she didn't want to keep on going."

I stopped for a minute, took a deep breath; then went on and told him the rest. "Jasper," I said. "I think my ma got stuck in her mind somewhere between her fine home in Kingston and our hills. Somehow, I think it just pulled her apart, like a raft breaking apart on rocks you can't see. She didn't fight dying much, not like that boy in Foul Rift."

"Sorry," Jasper said. "Real sorry, Hattie Belle."

"Yeah," I said. "Wished I'd known you before, Jasper."

"Me, too," he said.

After that, we didn't say one thing more.

Guess we were all glad that the next day was our last for this trip. Figured from the time we left till the time we got back home, it'd be leastways a week. Unless we got a lot of rain, the river would be a whole lot friendlier next trip down.

Pa piloted us on down to Trenton, didn't say a word about me steering now. I didn't have the heart for it anyhow.

When we tied up at Trenton, Pa said it was the end of

the line. We'd pay the extra to have a boat pilot our raft on to Philadelphia. He and Rastus collected the money, paid me and Jasper. That was something, having money of my own for the first time.

We set out for a hot meal at a nearby hotel. While we were eating, Rastus told us the change of plans. "Guess we won't go on to New York with you this trip, Amos," he said.

"New York?" I said. I looked across at Jasper. "But why not? How much longer could it take?"

"It's best; that's all," Rastus said. "Me and Jasper will walk to Port Jervis, catch the Erie Railroad to Hancock, walk the rest of the way from there."

I could tell Jasper was disappointed, but he didn't go against his pa. "Me and Pa will take the ropes and the tools," Jasper said. "No need for you to be weighted down with extra stuff."

"Thank you, son," Pa said. He patted Jasper on the shoulder. That was something. Pa said that he and I would leave on the next train going out to New York City, so I could see the big city and spend my wages.

I looked at Pa and Jasper and Rastus. Don't know why, exactly, but I got a feeling like they were privy to something I wasn't. Didn't care for that.

We started out for the train station after that. Pa and Rastus walked on ahead. That left me and Jasper alone.

"It won't be the same, you not going with us," I said.

Jasper bit his lip, pulled on the rim of his hat. "Guess you won't be buying a rifle," he said.

"I might, if you're still willing to teach me," I said.

"I am," Jasper said.

"That a promise?"

"Promise," Jasper said.

"All right then, I'll use Pa's," I said. We were outside the station now. Rastus went inside with Pa to buy our tickets. Jasper and I waited outside.

"Take off your hat, Hattie Belle," Jasper said.

I scowled. "Why on earth for?"

"Just do it," Jasper said.

I glanced around, doffed my hat, held it against my chest and smiled big at him, showed him all my teeth. "That good enough?"

"Yup," Jasper said, with a little grin. He took a step closer, leaned over, and whispered in my ear, "You're a pretty girl, Hattie Belle." He quick kissed my cheek and pulled back.

I pressed my palm against that cheek, pressing that kiss to keep forever.

"You come back safe, you hear?" Jasper blinked as if dust had flown into his eyes.

"Course I will," I said as Pa and Rastus came out of the station. "I'll see you in a couple of days. We got lots more trips to make."

Jasper nodded. Didn't say a word, just shouldered the rope Pa had been carrying. Rastus carried the tools in a gunnysack.

We parted company then. Pa and I boarded the passenger train for New York. Felt odd going on without Jasper.

"Don't feel much like going to the city, Pa," I said. "Guess that boy drowning made us all pretty sad."

"It did at that," Pa said.

We were quiet, thinking about the boy and his pa, I guess.

"You were like a hawk, Pa, flying straight and strong. You were really something."

"You were really something, too, Hattie," he said. "Your ma woulda been proud."

"Proud of you, too, Pa," I said.

After that, I looked at the pretty wood and curlicue iron, velvety soft seats. Stared out the window, listened to the rhythmic clicking of the wheels on the rails. Watched as we rushed past farms and villages and marshes, till I couldn't keep my eyes open any longer. I leaned my head against Pa's arm and went to sleep.

Pa woke me up when we reached the end of the line in New Jersey. We took the ferry across the Hudson to New York City.

"Stick close to me," Pa said, in warning.

Didn't have to tell me that twice. After our cabin on the mountain above Pepacton, everything seemed big and overpowering — the train station, the mansions, the hotels, the stores, and buildings climbing on top of each other nearly. People jostled and shouted, horses and carriages clattered on cobblestone streets, streetcars rattled and squealed on iron rails.

"Come on, littleun," Pa said, taking my hand. I didn't mind. We dodged and shuffled to avoid the throng, made our way from the ferry landing, walked across and then up, way up to Third Avenue and Fifty-sixth Street. It was calmer up here on the edge of the city. Guess I liked quiet better than I knew, just like Pa.

I'd had my fill of the city's noisy impatience by the time Pa stopped in front of a building rising five stories high. Pa told me it was a department store — Bloomingdale's. "Figured you'd be wanting a new dress, Hattie Belle," he said.

Looked up at Pa when he said that, had a little catch in my throat to swallow. "Ayah," I said, a happy flush warming my cheeks. "Guess that's why you brought me into the city."

Pa swallowed hard and half nodded, took me inside where there were acres of bins and counters of glass with all sorts of gadgets and goods, perfumes and jewelry, floors of furniture, and ready-made clothes. I never supposed there could be so much stuff in the entire world.

With Pa looking on, I picked a checked gingham dress the blue color of my eyes, high button boots and sturdy hose, a hat trimmed with flowers and lace. Pa added a satin parasol and a navy cloak to my purchases.

Then to my wonder, Pa picked himself a dark-plaid cutaway suit, percale shirt, bowler hat, and new boots. After Pa had everything wrapped up, he let me look around, going with me from department to department, floor to floor.

For myself, I chose a diary and a book called *The Lady of the Lake,* and for Jasper a book called *Robinson Crusoe.* He might not fancy reading a book, but I thought he'd like it just fine if I read it to him. I purchased a nice harmonica for Pa. Had a feeling Pa was ready to sing again like the old days. Had a feeling we might sing together.

And if Pa didn't feel like talking, I had a feeling he'd like playing a harmonica.

We took the *Mary Powell* steamship up the Hudson River. Could hardly wait to get home for Jasper and me to talk about New York.

When we were having supper, Pa said, "We're making a special trip tomorrow. Wanted to tell you b'fore. Didn't know how." Pa's eyes filled with pain like when Ma died.

I'd been thinking so hard about that poor boy and getting back home to see Jasper, that it took a second for Pa's words to set up an alarm.

Pa struggled, opened his mouth, shut it again, worried his fingers on the tablecloth. "Oh, hell," he said, striking the table with his fist. "I've taught you everything I know. Wanted to show you something about me that was good. I know you hated me. Don't blame you for that. Guess you had reason to think I didn't like you much. It wasn't what you thought . . ." Pa trailed off, swiped at his eyes. "You got that sweet, musical voice like your ma. Couldn't bear to hear it after . . . wasn't mad at you, it was me, going about everything wrong, not knowing how to fix the pain in either of us. Just turned me into a mean old cuss."

I didn't say a word, just sat and soaked in Pa's feelings, knowing they were my own. "Guess I turned into a mean old cuss, too."

Pa went on, "Don't want to ruin your life like I did your ma's."

"But I'm not Ma. I belong in the hills. I'm strong. Real strong, Pa."

"Ayah," he said, his face long with sadness.

A river of thought spun around in my head, floated together, fit into a pattern like logs and lash poles, pieces that shaped the story of our journey, mine and Pa's. "You taking me to Kingston, Pa?" I asked.

"Yup," he said. "Taking you to your grandma's."

"My grandma, she knows I'm coming . . . to stay," I said slowly. It wasn't a question; it was the answer.

"She knows you're coming," Pa said. "Had a letter writ for me by the lawyer in Downsville awhile after your ma died. Went down the night the big storm came to see if she'd sent a reply. There was."

Got a lump the size of a walnut in my throat, swallowed hard, remembered Pa's sad look. Recalled how ornery I'd been, too. "Why didn't you tell me, Pa?"

"Couldn't. Thought she might change her mind about

you, decide she didn't want you like she did your ma after she took up with me. Guess your grandma's had her fill of being unforgiving."

"She won't like me," I said.

"Reckon I can't guarantee that, Hattie Belle. She'll get you a good schooling, teach you proper ways. It's what your ma wanted for you."

"Ma? What she wanted for me? Ma quit on me, Pa. Quit trying to get well."

Pa took a jagged breath. Still looked sad. "She quit on me, too."

"Are you quitting on me?" I asked.

"Ain't quitting on you, Hattie Belle. Won't quit on you, even to my last damn fighting breath, not now, not ever. Just want you to get the schooling like your ma wanted. Don't want you to stay in Kingston one minute longer, unless you want to."

In the morning, our boat docked at the port in Rhinecliff. We ferried across to Rondout by Kingston, and Pa found us a place to get a bath and change into our new clothes. Felt like I wasn't suited to such fine fashion, but I liked it. Made me feel like a real girl again, a different girl, older somehow. The hat covered up the evidence of my short hair.

"Look like a real belle," Pa said. He stopped and looked at me again like he was seeing me for the first time. "Why . . . you've grown up on me, sure enough. Look pretty as your ma ever did when she was gussied up in her fancy gown." Pa rubbed his chin like he was studying up on something.

"What you thinking now, Pa?" I asked. I smoothed my skirt and admired the ruffles.

"I'm thinking we got us one more stop to make before we go . . ." Pa took me up to a grand place. "See that fancy hotel? That's where I met your ma."

"And where you danced?"

"That's where we danced all right."

"And you sang to her. She said you sang to her. Did you sing 'Red River Valley'?"

"Sang her a different song — the one about the blackbird and the maid with golden hair."

"That was a good one, Pa. Right for Ma."

"Ayah," Pa said.

We went into the hotel and Pa talked to a man there. The man smiled, led me and Pa to a ballroom with large pillars, creamy plaster flowers cascading down the walls, crystal chandeliers. It was empty and silent.

Pa crooked his arm. "Come here, girl," he said.

155

He took me to the center of the floor, showed me all the steps of a waltz. And then we danced, Pa in his cutaway coat and I in my gingham gown. He whirled me gracefully like he was made to dance the way he was made to swing an ax, walk on water. First, he counted one, two, three, one, two, three, so I could keep in step. Like Pa, the steps came natural to me.

Then he sang, changing the song to match the dance:

> *"From this valley they say you are going,*
> *I will miss your bright eyes and sweet smile.*
> *For they say you are taking the sunshine*
> *That has brightened my pathway awhile."*

Then I understood. "Red River Valley" was for me, my song, my very own.

"You'll always be my girl, Hattie Belle," Pa said, when the dancing was done.

"Ayah," I said. *My girl.* Pa said it. *My girl.* Guess that was the closest we could come to letting on to our deeper feelings. This time I didn't wait. I grabbed Pa's hand, and he held it fast.

Chapter Twenty-one

I thought Pa and me made a fine-looking pair, walking up to the big house where Ma used to live, where she grew up. Didn't feel a bit ordinary. Felt a little quivery, sitting in the fancy drawing room and being served tea in china cups, and eating sugared cakes while I studied my grandma.

She was a little gray bird with weak eyes and a musical voice. She spoke with sweet words and sugary smiles to me, but there was a coldness in Grandma like a deep frost in the ground whenever she looked at Pa. Living here would make my former lot in life seem like a frolic. Grandma would have lots of rules to obey, more than in school.

Pa shuffled his feet and worried his hat and looked at my grandma like he was pleading for something.

"Amos, you know that *I* will give Hattie the best care," she said.

"I know it," Pa said, but he still had that pleading look.

"I don't believe that you and I have any other business. Do we?" Grandma said, standing up.

"I guess not," he said, lowering his eyes from her face.

Pa didn't tarry. Didn't blame him. Knew he had lots of work ahead of him. I felt some comfort, knowing Jasper would be with Pa on the river, but Pa still had to get an extra hand.

I followed Pa out to the sidewalk, though Grandmother — as she had already instructed me to address her — gave me a disapproving look.

"Don't want to stay here, Pa," I said, my lip trembling.

"Don't want you to neither, Hattie Belle, but you know it's best, know it's right, at least for now."

I didn't cry but I tasted blood from biting my lip. I gave him the book for Jasper and Ma's diary to keep for me, and the harmonica. "Figured you might play this sometimes, since you're not much given to talk."

"Guess I will at that. Won't know what to do without the chipmunk chatter." He blinked and started to turn away, but I grabbed his sleeve.

"I'll always be a Hill Hawk, no matter what," I said fiercely.

"I know it, Hattie Belle. You got spirit. Reckon you always will." Then he left, waving when he got to the end of the lane.

I whistled once, long and high and shrill. I waited, and it came, Pa's hawk whistle came back to me like an echo, like he was at the edge of the clearing waiting for me. Then he was gone.

I turned and stared up at the snow-white house with its fancy lattices and gingerbread and heavy windows. I took a deep breath and started up the walk. I was Hattie Belle Basket, a Hill Hawk. Guess if I could journey down an angry river, I could scale a sugared fortress.

"There you are," my grandmother chirped from the doorway.

"Yes, Grandmother, I'm right here." I walked up, took her hand, smiled into her frosty eyes.

My true home was not far away, not as far away as forever like Ma had said about hers, but near enough for me to go to when it was time. Pa would be waiting and Jasper, too. They wouldn't quit on me, and I wouldn't quit on them. Next to that, nothing else mattered.

In 1764, twelve years prior to the Declaration of Independence, Daniel Skinner of Damascus, Pennsylvania, cut, trimmed, and built a raft of timbers, which he floated down the Delaware River from Bush's Eddy near Callicoon, New York, to market in Philadelphia. Thus began a more than century-long industry that saw its heyday in the decade between 1875 to 1885.

During the days of the rafting industry, the water level of the river and its tributaries was much higher than today. Heavy growth of timber in the unsettled mountainous areas kept the sun from drying out the ground. The timber was cut indiscriminately, much of it was left to rot, and the second growth, which lacked the proper moist conditions of the virgin forests, could not grow to the height or girth of the former.

What seemed to be an inexhaustible commodity was not. By the time of Hattie's story, much of the timber had already been harvested, leaving many of the once-forested mountains bare, eroded, and unlovely. Today, we understand the importance of our natural resources, our rivers, our streams, our forests and wildlife, and our own intrinsic part in preservation. But it was a different time, a different way of life, and logging and rafting were the means of survival for the Hill Hawks of the upper east branch of the Delaware River.

⊰ ACKNOWLEDGMENTS ⊱

*I'm thankful to the following people and institutions, who
helped me in my research and in so many other ways:*

Shirley Keesler, at the WSPL, Callicoon Branch, for assistance and moral support.

Mary Curtis for sharing the work of Charles T. Curtis, Esq.

Kay Parisi and Jane Walker, at the Downsville Central School Library, for assistance.

Delhi Elementary Library, Delhi, New York, for providing out-of-print materials.

Ann Foster, at the Wayne County Public Library, for assistance.